YOU'RE STILL HERE

EMMA THOMAS

<u>With a gracious heart</u>, I would like to dedicate this book to my husband, David, and our wonderful children, Brooke & Xander. Thank you for always believing in me, and never letting me doubt myself.

Also, to my dear friends, Caitlin & Nicole, my sister-in-law, Jade & my sister, Christina. Thank you all for everything. Without you, I cannot imagine ever finishing this book.

And, of course, Lisa Hunter. I always told you that someday I would dedicate my first book to you, I'm just sorry it took so long.

Chapter 1

~ Dismissed and Disbelieved ~

Light spilled into the classroom from the only window in the room. It was the kind of brilliant sunlight that only happens after a long, dark storm, and it was now setting fire to the white walls with its golden glow. The afternoon had been disrupted by the loud slapping of rain against the windows, sudden flashes of lightning breaking across the thick, gloomy sky, and the booming of thunder overhead.

Having been distracted by the storm, the students had only completed a few of their lessons in the forty-seven minutes since the class had started, but most were working quietly at their desks. But even now, after the cloak of low clouds had lifted, and the thunder had passed beyond earshot, there was a tapping on the window from a tree branch stuck in the light breeze outside that was pulling Liam's attention away from his worksheet.

Late autumn storms passing over the vast, open skies above the town of Larsen Creek were rare, especially in late October. The usual weather for this time of year was windy and dry, causing the many trees in town to shed their leaves and the grass to turn grey in preparation for the dead of the long winter that was now on the threshold. People who lived in the area would often joke that they only ever had two seasons-eight months of winter and four months of road construction, which was usually proven true year after year.

Larsen Creek was thoughtfully named because of the creek that ran through the middle of town, which by late fall was now barely a trickled whisper down the trenched-out, rocky creek bed. The name Larsen was after the Larsen family of London, England, who had come to Canada sometime in the early eighteen hundreds and had built the town around them. Many people in town still carried the name, and many businesses were named after the family.

There was only one place to find steady work: the Larsen Saw Mill, just on the outskirts of the small town. Most of the people who lived here had worked at the mill in some capacity or another at some time or another. The town was comfortably nestled between two hillsides and surrounded by farmland and thick forests. It was small enough to walk from one end to the other in less than an hour, with one highway in and the same highway out, and its citizens grew old, dreaming of leaving someday.

"Well," a voice thundered from behind the desk at the front of the room. "I guess when you stop expecting and start accepting, life becomes a lot easier!" Mrs. Hag scolded her English class in a frenzy of frustration that the end of the day was near and not one of her students had turned in their lesson. Liam turned his attention to the front of the class, looking over at the large desk Mrs. Hag sat behind, watching as she sat down again and began wrestling with a pen in her hand while marking papers from the day before, her mouth twisted with frustration.

Liam's eyes followed the stacks of unmarked homework that built a wall along the edge of the desk, and then the name plaque that sat on the front of it caught his eyes. Liam thought about the first time he'd ever met her. She had only come to the school this year and had assigned an entire homework booklet on the first day of classes, expecting it to be completed and turned in the next day.

"Mrs. Hag. Well, it is a pretty accurate name for her," he continued to himself. "I wonder how hard it must be to teach with a name like Mrs. Hag." He let his thoughts continue to wander. "To have a name that perfectly describes who you are as a person, without even having to go past introductions. Mrs. Hag, indeed." Straight away, Liam felt a slight tinge of guilt over the thought. He had no idea what made Mrs. Hag so miserable; for all he knew, she could have a good reason for it. His mother used to tell him never to judge anyone too harshly because no one could ever be sure of what silent battles others might be facing, and now Liam could hear her voice in his head scolding him for such an awful thought. He quickly looked down at his paper, not wanting her to catch him staring at the front of the room as she looked up from her desk.

Mrs. Hag stood up again and surveyed the classroom; her brows were down nearly to the bridge of her nose, and her right hand was so tightly grasped to the mug that held her cold coffee that Liam thought the handle might break off. "Anything you do not complete today I will be expecting in my hand, complete, first thing tomorrow," she informed. With that, the classroom broke out into groans of upset tenth graders, their worlds nearly ending with the very mention of homework.

"Hush, and get back to your lesson!" Mrs. Hag demanded, and the classroom fell quiet again.

Liam tapped the eraser end of his pencil quietly on his desk as his eyes were drawn back to the window, now looking past the tree caught in the breeze and up the street. In the distance, Liam could see a familiar four-door car, affectionally named 'Ol' Rusty, parked on the side of the road just up from the school. Liam sat straight up from his desk, his back cracking as it lengthened away from his hard chair. He exhaled all the breath from his lungs out of his nose with a long sigh, as he felt his nerves settle deep in his stomach.

Even from as far as the class window, he could see Ol' Rusty's weathered paint and worn parts, and leaning against the unpolished, sun-faded hood was his oldest brother, Drew, who was waiting for the school bell to ring.

Liam was the youngest of three brothers, but anyone who saw the three together would tell you that he looked out of place next to the others. Liam's curly dark hair and dark eyes were in stark contrast to those of his older brothers, Drew and Jacob, with their straight blonde hair and bright blue eyes; these were the only things their father ever gave them. Liam would often wonder when people would comment on how much he looked like their mother if his brothers held resentment towards him because of it, and would always brush off any comments from people about it when either of his brothers were around.

Liam would only see Drew when he dropped by unannounced, which, until lately, was few and far between. Drew had moved out of the house nearly two years before, jumping from couch to couch of anywhere that would have him, and sometimes, when he had worn out all of his welcomes, he would have to sleep in the backseat of Ol' Rusty. Although Drew would tell anyone who would listen that their father kicked him out, the boy's father would say that Drew left in a storm of anger and never moved back. Although Liam would never say it to anyone, he often felt that home was never the same after Drew had left.

Liam glanced at the clock above the door, watching the second hand as it crept slowly around. The classroom was still quiet, with nothing but the sound of the branch still tapping away on the window and the shuffle of the occasional foot under a desk. Thankfully, just as Liam had looked back at his worksheet, the school bell finally rang. Mrs. Hag again told her class her expectations for the start of class the next day before demanding the students not to race her to the door as she was leaving. Liam grabbed his bag from the back of his chair, took the incomplete work off his desk, and, with the other students, poured out into the hallways.

The school hallway was Liam's favorite place in the entire school because it was the only place he could catch a few minutes with Nick between classes and, if they were lucky, after school. Nick Foster was Liam's only friend, and they had been inseparable since they had met in first grade, where they first bonded over their love for kites. Since that first day, Liam knew he had found a lifelong ally in Nick, and together, they faced those hard years in those hallways. Unfortunately, this year, they did not have any of the same classes together for the first time in all their school years, so between classes was the only time they could catch up throughout the day.

Liam was excited as he scanned up and down the hallway for Nick. He had not seen him yet, as Nick had been late to school due to a late morning dentist appointment.

"Liam!" He heard called from behind him. He was reasonably sure that it was Nick bobbing his head over the crowds of kids across the hallway and waving his arms as he tried to push past people like a fish against the water flow.

As he got closer, Liam felt more confident that it was Nick approaching- or at least some version of him. Liam tried his best to extinguish a laugh when he saw what Nick was wearing. Although he was no longer surprised by Nick's daily attempts to fit in, sometimes these attempts were too funny not to laugh. Before the start of tenth grade, Nick had worn mostly cargo pants and long, plain tee shirts, and was never worried about what anyone thought about his clothes. But on this day, Nick had on a black, oversized shirt with a gruesome tableau of absolute carnage, with twisted figures in agonizing poses, splattered blood, and in the middle with what was made up of dripping, bloody-looking font was a logo for a band that Liam had never heard of; and he knew Nick's parents well enough to know just by the look of the shirt that there was no way that his parents would have let him listen to them, either.

Nick struggled as he shuffled towards Liam. The bottoms of his baggy black pants were dragging on the floor under his feet, and on them was a chain hanging down to his knees from one belt loop to another. All his black hair was spiked up in rows, and he had thick black bracelets locked on his wrists and spikes across his neck. He also noticed that Nick was not wearing his glasses, which Liam guessed was why he was bumping into other kids as he walked towards him.

The fact was, Liam never cared how Nick dressed; he could have come to school wearing a cardboard box, and Liam would proudly walk down the hallways next to him. His only worry was that he was trying too hard to change who he was to fit in, and not being true to himself. The day before, which happened to be a Wednesday, Nick came to school dressed in a black button-up shirt and dress pants, his hair slicker than an oil spill as it clung tightly to his head and swept back like it had just been combed a moment before. Every few minutes, he would say, "Wednesday's child is full of woe," like this was some profound poetry, and he, in turn, was deep for reciting it.

Nick was more intelligent than the average tenth grader, spending his free time coding computer software in his basement. In all the time Liam had known him, he had never worried too much about what anyone thought about him or when the other kids would bug him about his intelligence. Liam was a bit jealous of his friend's smarts in some ways, as it kept the bullies at bay. Instead of beating him, they just made him do their homework for them, which was better than some of the other kids got off. However, this year, he worked hard to hide his smarts from the other kids so they might like him more. To delicately quote Nick's father, because, 'no one likes a smartass.' However, the harder Nick tried to make a good impression on the other kids, the more unlikable they found him. He would change his hair and clothes. He would even try on different personalities occasionally just to try to fit in, but the more he tried, the more desperate and pathetic he came across.

Liam never understood how the other kids did not see what he saw in Nick, and in some ways, he was thankful that they did not. Nick was always a good friend to him. He was intelligent and funny and never asked too many questions about Liam's home life, which suited him fine. Selfishly, Liam felt that if he ever actually fit in with the other kids, Nick might never look back to the kid he flew kites with in elementary.

"How's it going?" Liam asked.

"Oh, ya know," Nick groaned in an irregular tone, "another great day of barely hanging by a thread!"

The two walked down the busy hallway together toward their lockers. "What do you call this look?" Liam teased. "What band is that on your shirt?"

"I have no idea; it's my older brothers," Nick looked at him, only now noticing the tinge of sarcasm in his comment. "Stop making fun. Besides, this is what all the other kids are wearing." Nick made a hand gesture to the kids around them. Liam looked all around, but there was not another kid with clothes that came close to how his friend was dressed, so he was unsure to whom Nick was referring. "Besides, so get this," Nick said, a built-up excitement in his voice that bellowed out all at once, "I've decided I'm going to ask out Holly Dunham," Nick announced, stretching his hand out to Liam for a high-five.

Liam gave him a lazy high-five back. "But didn't you just ask out Charlene?" He asked, a smile hinting at the corner of his mouth.

"Yeah, so?" Nick responded.

"As in Charlene Dunham?" Liam questioned, hoping that the not-so-subtle hint would be enough for Nick to realize what the problem was, but to no surprise, he did not. Nick had never been one to pick up on any social cues that were offered to him. "Don't you think that Holly might think it's weird that you asked out her sister last week, and now you're asking her out?"

"No, not at all. Charlene said no," Nick replied with a serious look on his face. "Besides, if Holly says no, I think I'll just ask out Michelle Bradford! And besides, my older brother told me that most girls like to play hard to get, so even if Holly says no, asking out her sister might actually make Charlene jealous enough to go out with me. He called it 'basic math' or something."

"Oh yeah?" Liam laughed, "And who will you ask if Charlene and Michelle both say no and Holly doesn't get jealous?" Liam tried to think of how he could better explain to Nick that systematically asking each girl out until one said yes probably was not the best way to get a first girlfriend, but he could not find the words. "*Just throwing against a wall and hoping that something sticks,*" or "*casting a dragnet,*" was all that came to mind, but he knew Nick would not understand these references. Hope sprang eternal in Nick's eyes, and who was

Liam to dim that for his friend? *"Some lessons are best learned the hard way,"* he thought.

Nick shook his head and shrugged off the sting of his friend's continued teasing, and a look of pity fell over his face, as if not to say that it was not Liam's fault that he did not know how to get a girlfriend. "Besides, my brother has had, like, four girlfriends in the past three months, and this is what he says works. So, you can talk to him about it! Actually, do you want to come to my house today? We could tell your dad we have a project for school or something. Then you can ask my brother yourself." Nick suggested.

"We don't even have any classes together," Liam laughed again.

"As if your dad knows that," Nick laughed back, pulling his pants up that were dragging so far on the ground that other kids were stepping on them.

Liam shrugged and nodded. "Yeah, you're probably right about that. But I can't today, anyway. I saw Drew parked out front. I'm guessing he wants to hang out with me and Jacob."

"All good," Nick responded. "Maybe next time! See ya, Liam!" Before Liam could answer, Nick had turned down another hallway toward his locker and was out of sight.

By the time Liam had reached his locker, the hallways had become even louder as kids met up with all their friends, forming large groups around the halls. He closed his locker door after grabbing his coat off the hook inside and set off to find Jacob. Liam continued his walk down the long white hallway lined with rows and rows of red lockers, his thumbs hooked under the straps on his backpack, trying not to trip over the uneven tiles that made up the hallway floors. Over his head was that flickering of half-burnt lights, and the smell of the left-over lunch in the cafeteria was always in the air at this time of day. Budget cuts to the school district over recent years had left the school with more repairs than there was money to fix, and it was only at the end of the day, when the light came through the windows in just the wrong way, all the disrepair of the building came into sight at the same time.

Liam walked past Jacob's locker with no sign of him, but he could hear a commotion further up the hallway. He started walking towards the noise, but it was not until he was a few steps away that he recognized his brother Jacob's voice mixed with all the yelling. Liam's eyes rolled as he walked faster toward the noise, pushing through a circle of kids that surrounded a small group. In the middle of the circle was Jacob, who was on the ground with the back of his head pressed against the bottom of a row of lockers and had his face covered by his arms. Towering over Jacob was Steven Farlow, with both hands squeezed into tight fists at his side. Jacob uncovered his face, looking up from the ground. He wiped the blood from his lip onto his sleeve and then spat the blood from his mouth at Steven, covering his white shoes with red specks.

Steven Farlow was not the smartest or wealthiest kid in school. Still, he was known to be one of the coolest kids at the school only because of his broad, mountain shoulders, blue cord veins that tied down both of his arms, and being the only student with a five o'clock shadow by the time the afternoon lunch bell rang each day. Everyone in school knew you would have to be an idiot to mess with him.

Chapter 2

~ Black Eyes ~

"What an idiot!" Liam whispered to himself, feeling suddenly clammy and hot as he tried to decide if he should jump in to help his brother. "Of course Jacob would pick a fight with the biggest kid at school!"

Liam was not very big, and he could not put up much of a fight at that, but he knew that Jacob would not win in a fight against this kid alone. Liam pulled up his sleeves over his forearms as he waited for a decision to come to him. As he looked around the circle, other boys around Steven shouted and cheered him on, grabbing him by the shoulders in excitement. Others were just shouting and were not cheering anyone on in particular. Liam tightened each of his hands into a fist, his fingernails digging into the palm of his sweaty hands, his heart beating so fast it was tripping over itself.

Jacob did not see Liam as he jumped up from the floor, leaving his backpack where it had fallen beside him. Liam was unsure if he would have cared if he had seen him since Jacob, as well as anyone, knew that Liam would not be the first to jump into any fight or dangerous situation. Before Jacob's feet were back under him, he rushed towards Steven, whose hands were now pulled back and ready to throw another punch.

"Jacob!" Liam cried out, stepping closer without a thought other than trying to reach Jacob before he got himself even more hurt. Liam was unsure if Jacob had not heard him call out to him or if he had not cared to look as he charged. Just as Liam stepped closer, the hallway was filled with the sound of Mr. Doyle's custom-made, orthotic black soles screeching to an abrupt stop, and he was now stomping towards them. Pushing his way through the wall of kids, Mr. Doyle's face was hot with anger, and he was almost snorting as he stormed closer. "Jacob Robertson!" Mr. Doyle shouted, "What is the meaning of this?!" the kids scattered as Mr. Doyle stepped between the two boys, his hands prying at Jacob's as he tried loosening the grip that Jacob now had on the collar of Steven's coat.

Jacob stepped back and looked at Mr. Doyle, his eyes shooting daggers, "are you serious? Did you even see what *he* did?" Jacob took another step back, wiping the blood off his split lip onto the sleeve of his sweater. "Steven hit me! I didn't even touch him!"

Mr. Doyle grabbed Jacob by a fist full of the hood of his sweater and began towing him away from Steven and down the hallway. Liam grabbed Jacob's backpack, which had been left on the hallway floor, and trailed behind them. Steven trailed behind Liam.

"Let me go! I'm fine!" Jacob shouted, trying to shake Mr. Doyle's hold on him as they walked.

Now, it must be said that Mr. Doyle, although a decent enough science teacher, was not a good mediator and was not equipped to handle the situation he had found himself in. Hesitantly and wishing that another teacher would take charge of the situation, Mr. Doyle let go, giving Jacob a shove, but he continued walking between the two. They walked down the hallway and towards the front entrance. Jacob continued to receive the occasional shove on his shoulder from Mr. Doyle every time he glanced back at Steven, who now, out of Mr. Doyle's sight, was making mocking faces at Jacob from behind them. As soon as Jacob was out of Mr. Doyle's reach, he launched back at Steven and punched him square in the face. Steven fell to the ground, cupping his face in his palms.

"Jacob!" Mr. Doyle yelled again, scrambling as he tried to regain his grip on his coat. Jacob grabbed his backpack from Liam, kicked the front entrance door open, and walked out without a word. "Your father will be hearing about this!" was all that Mr. Doyle could think to say as the front door slammed closed behind Jacob and Liam. "Don't be surprised when he gets a call regarding your suspension… maybe even expulsion!" He added.

Liam caught up to Jacob a few steps down from the front entrance, looking back to see if Mr. Doyle was following them. "Drew is waiting for us," Liam said, taking two steps to Jacob's one, trying to catch up to him. Jacob did not even pause to acknowledge that Liam was talking to him. "Jacob, wait up. Do you want to talk about it?" Liam asked, now running to follow him. "What happened?"

"Just the same old same. Apparently, some guys on the basketball team think I'm ugly, so they punched me in the face." Jacob replied through his bloody teeth.

"Well, you should probably find some ice to put on that. You're bleeding."

"Thanks, tips," Jacob mocked, again wiping his lip onto his blood-stained sleeve.

The two brothers walked quickly, keeping their heads down and not looking at the row of vehicles full of smiling parents as they greeted their children. Liam knew Jacob felt the same envy burn as they walked past them each day, so he said nothing to Jacob, knowing that no matter the intentions behind them, any words would just add fuel to that burn, and Jacob would snap at him. Drew would never park where the other kids got picked up and was a little way down the next street.

"Ready to go, boys?" Drew asked, patting the car's hood and dusting up a cloud of dirt and rust into the air.

"Do we have to?" Jacob groaned, tightening the backpack strap onto his shrugging shoulders.

"Oh, come on, Jacob," Drew laughed. "If I hadn't shown up to pick you up, you'd just be sitting in your room, sulking about nothing. Look at your face. Who'd you piss off this time?"

Jacob rolled his eyes and jumped into the back seat, the door squeaking as it opened and squeaking even louder as it closed. Drew smiled at Liam as if not to say that he had won the argument and went to follow Jacob into the car.

"Mr. Robertson!" A familiar, condescending voice boomed from behind the car.

"Ah, would you look at that," Drew snarled, a grin across his face as he hung his head out of the car window. "Principal Johnson, you walk all the way over here to tell me you miss me?"

Principal Johnson was an unhappy man by nature. Although the kids at the school often rumored that he lived in a one-bedroom apartment with *only* the four cats to keep him company, the truth, as it usually is, was much sadder. Principal Johnson lived alone in a three-bedroom house that his wife, after taking the kids, had left him in ten years before, saying he drank too much and cared too little. The years had made him sour, and everyone who knew him was surprised that he chose education as a profession. Principal Johnson never liked kids, but disliked the three Robertson brothers the most. Drew had once had the entire school laughing when he had toilet-papered Principal Johnson's car, which left the already bitter old man disgruntled and unforgiving. Drew was kicked out of school that day, leaving the two younger brothers to pay the price for what everyone in school called the "total wipe out" of the principal's pride. He stood with his arms crossed tightly across his puffed chest, looking down his nose at the three brothers. Even standing in the high sun of the afternoon, his grey hair against his grey skin, Principal Johnson looked so depleted and utterly devoid of any colour that he seemed grey all over.

"I just had a rather interesting conversation with Mr. Doyle about your brother, Jacob. I suggest you boys keep out of trouble now. I'll already be making one call to your father. I'd hate to have to report that all three of his delinquents are causing trouble in one day." Principal Johnson glared through his thin-rimmed glasses with a smirk. The light shone off the bald spot on top of his head that was hardly, but carefully, hidden beneath a few strains of combed-over grey hairs.

"Oh, come on," Drew interrupted, saying through his smile, "You just live for making trouble for us, don't you, Principal J?" With a satisfied grin, Drew left in what Principal Johnson would refer to as 'pealing out' in his incident notebook he always kept tucked in his left jacket pocket next to his ballpoint pen.

The inside of Drew's car was worse off than the outside. The smell of stinking, old, wet socks burned through Liam's nose and into his eyes. Fast food wrappers and water bottles carpeted the floor and crunched underneath their feet. Drew scanned through the static on the radio, trying to find something to drown out the silence in the car, and finally settled on a classic rock station.

"So, Liam, how's school going?" Drew asked, turning the radio volume down a notch.

"It's fine," Liam answered.

"Got any girlfriends yet?" Drew laughed.

"Nope," Liam answered again. Liam felt a tinge of guilt pulse through him. He could tell that Drew was making an honest attempt to try to make conversation and that in his short replies, he could be read that he was not interested in talking to him at all. It was not that Liam did not like his brother; it was just that the years had pulled the two apart, and now it felt almost like a disruption any time Drew would stop in unannounced. What was worse for Liam was that Drew would never really take a no for an answer when it came to the boys spending time with him when he showed up. But what bothered Liam the most was how Drew always seemed to pick a fight with Jacob at some point during their visits. Liam felt that if anyone in the family would even try to do their part to keep the peace, they could have a chance at a happy family- or what was left of their family. He craved the simple days when everyone got along, and the three brothers felt like they were on the same team, them against the world. Now, whenever Drew was around, Liam could feel a change come over Jacob as thick anxiety fell across him, making everyone and every situation and interaction tense.

"How's dad been?" Drew asked, still trying.

Liam said nothing but let out a sigh through his nose, looking back at Jacob, who was sitting silently in the backseat with his headphones on and his eyes hidden beneath the brim of his hood.

"Huh," Drew remarked, "that bad, hey?"

Again, Liam did not answer. He knew that anything he said about their dad was not a conversation worth having with Drew. In truth, Liam wished that he had someone to talk to about his dad. Jacob was in the trenches with him at home, and his burden was just as heavy as Liam's. As for Drew, Liam felt he never had anything good or helpful to add to the conversations and would get so riled up that he would end up wishing he had never said anything. On top of that, Liam knew that Jacob felt Drew had abandoned them when he left home and that talking about their dad would somehow spin out of control into a spitting match between the two older brothers. That's what had happened the last few times, anyway. So, Liam did not answer.

"Check this out," Drew stretched his arm out, reaching under Liam's legs and under the garbage on the passenger-side floor, keeping a barely steady hand on the steering wheel as he did. He pulled up a dense chunk of metal with a glass top. Inside were red and blue lights and wires hanging off of it. The bottom metal was rusting, and rust flakes covered Liam's lap as Drew dropped it on him.

"What is that?" Liam asked as he picked it up. "It looks like a fake police light.

"It's not fake," Drew insisted. "It's just an old one. Junko gave it to me from an old car he had on his property and traded it for work I did for him.

"Does it work?" Liam asked.

"You bet it does!"

"What do you use it for?"

"Well, I haven't used it yet, but I'm sure that it'll come in handy someday."

Liam placed the light back onto the floor carefully so that it would not land on his toes.

"What about you, Jacob? Finally make any friends this year?" Drew laughed.

Liam glanced back, hoping Jacob would catch the sympathetic look Liam was flashing in response to Drew's rude question. But Jacob never looked up, and Liam hoped that Jacob never heard the question or the laugh at all.

"So where do you guys go to find pop cans for old man Lister these days?" Drew asked. "I could use some extra cash to throw some gas into Ol' Rusty. I was thinking about hitting up the school cafeteria but figured they wouldn't let me pass the front doors. I thought you guys might have another spot."

"We usually just go to the mill," Liam answered. "Jacob goes every day." Liam looked back at Jacob, hoping he would not be upset that he had told Drew that. When Jacob gave no response, Liam continued, "Sometimes the office ladies will just give us the entire recycling."

"Well, that's where we'll go," Drew announced, heavily pressing his foot on the gas. Ol' Rusty slowly roared up to speed.

The mill was clearly marked with no trespassing signs, but the boys came often enough and never caused any trouble; the workers would just leave them be. Outside the main buildings and out of the line of workers was a stretch of train cars along the tracks leading out of the mill. The train cars were lined up in rows along two tracks, and the boys liked to look at all the graffiti that covered them.

"Jacob," Drew called out. "Do you want to go to the office and ask for the cans? If they give you some, we can split the money."

"You go!" Jacob snapped back. "I want to walk up here and look at the art."

Drew turned to Liam, which Liam knew meant that he would have to go and ask for the cans and meet Drew and Jacob when he was done. Liam did not argue the point. He knew that he was more likely to sweet-talk the office ladies into giving them the recycling than Drew would be. Off he strolled towards the office door as Drew and Jacob continued down the tracks.

Pat was working in the office, and Liam knew as soon as he saw her behind the desk, she would give him all the cans and bottles she could find. Pat was not an overly generous woman, nor did she have a big heart for charity; she had, however, known the boy's mother and thought this to be a way she would look out for them, even if it was just a tiny gesture.

Walking back from the office with a large bag full of cans, Liam looked for Jacob and Drew, who had wandered off between some parked trains and were out of sight. Liam looked at the ground and saw Jacob's footprints in the mud. He walked along them until he could hear shouting echoing off the train cars in front of him.

"Here we go," Liam muttered to himself. It was no surprise to him that the two were not getting along. Even when the boys were young, Jacob and Drew would fight so often that their mother would have to separate them, making Liam sit between them on car rides and even at the dinner table.

"This is why I don't tell you anything!" Jacob shouted while reaching to grab a white envelope from Drew's hand. "I don't trust you! Give it back!"

Drew lifted the paper from his brother's reach and pushed him onto the ground, laughing as Jacob fell into the mud.

"What is going on?" Liam interjected.

"Oh, Liam, you're gonna love this!" Drew laughed, lifting the paper in hand as high as he could and waving it in the air. "I just found out what Jacob's been doing when he comes here every day! You're seriously not going to believe this!"

Chapter 3

~Family Fractures~

To Drew, almost everything was a joke or something to be laughed at. On the surface, Drew was a young man who refused to take anything seriously, laughed when he should not, and was often insensitive. However, if anyone had taken the time to dig a bit deeper, they'd find in Drew a young man who was never equipped to deal with the weight of what the world had placed on him and hid his pain in laughter. But the truth was that even if anyone had tried to, Drew would never let anyone that close to him.

Jacob was quickly back on his feet. The back of his legs and back were covered in mud and were soaking onto his skin. Jacob's jaw was clenched so tight he could not even yell at Drew; his envelope was still waving in Drew's hand like a white flag. Liam could see sharp and straight handwritten letters on the front of it. Drew was still too busy laughing to notice Jacob walking towards him, and before he could react, Jacob grabbed the envelope, shoving Drew with his shoulder, and quickly started walking back up the tracks towards the yard gate.

Liam waited until Jacob was out of sight before he turned back to Drew. "What happened? What are you guys even fighting about? A piece of paper?"

Drew was still laughing and struggling to find his breath so he could speak. "Jacob has been coming down here every day writing letters to a pen pal," Drew answered, holding his stomach that had now cramped under his laughter. "A pen pal he's never even met!" Drew started laughing uncontrollably again. Liam stared blankly at Drew, wondering what he found funny, and figured he must be missing something.

"Well, I'm going to see if he's okay," Liam dropped the bag of cans beside Drew. "We'll just meet you at Mr. Lister's."

Liam saw Jacob as he passed the metal fence marking the entrance to the mill yard and caught up to him as he was grabbing his backpack from Drew's car. He slammed the car door as hard as he could before walking off.

The two walked for a block until Liam spoke. "I don't get what happened."

Jacob said nothing, dragging his heavy, muddy shoes up the sidewalk in long scrapes. Liam looked over at Jacob. The back of his sweater and pants were muddy and wet.

"Jacob, take my jacket. You can't go see Mr. Lister with mud all over you. He'll ask what happened to you," Liam took his coat from his backpack and offered it to Jacob. "You know how he worries about us."

"I don't care, let him," Jacob replied, trying to wipe some dirt off, getting his hands muddy as he tried. "He probably already knows what a jerk Drew is, anyway."

"Just take it." Liam again handed Jacob his coat, and reluctantly, Jacob took it. Jacob stopped to remove his muddy sweater, putting it into his backpack before putting on the coat and placing the now crimped envelope into the side pocket. "Now, can you just talk to me? Can you please tell me about this friend that Drew finds so funny?"

"Why?" Jacob asked, pulling up the jacket's zipper under his chin and throwing the hood over his head. "So you and Drew can have a good laugh about it later? Save me the time and go ask him!"

"No, Jacob," Liam insisted. "Because I care. Do you really think I'm like that?"

"No, I don't, Liam," Jacob sighed, and his tone shifted. Even in his anger, Jacob knew that Liam was not *'like that.'* "I just don't know how to explain it without sounding stupid."

"Well, just try. I promise I won't make fun of you. I just want to know."

To Liam's surprise, Jacob's face was filled with relief. His eyes softened as he looked at Liam. The sincerity in Liam's voice had broken the tension, and although still hesitant, Jacob slowly began to explain.

"You know how I've always liked the train car art? Well, I started taking pictures of it here last year, and I started noticing some of the art with the same signature. Here, look," Jacob said, stopping as he grabbed his camera from the front of his backpack. Jacob scanned through the photos in his camera, showing Liam all the pictures of the train art he had taken. One picture was of a giant octopus stretching along the side of an entire train car and one of a balloon with a house inside floating in a nicely painted sky. Jacob stopped on one of a mushroom with a door on it that was open to what looked like a galaxy. Jacob zoomed the screen into the right corner of this picture to what Liam could see Jacob was referring to as a signature, but Liam could not make out what it read; it looked like a mash-up of different letters into one signature, not like a name, but more like initials into a symbol.

"B-T-N?" Liam asked. "Is that what that says?" Liam asked again, trying to appear to Jacob that he was more interested than he actually was to keep him talking. "Are those someone's initials?"

"Yes, they are the artist's initials, I think. Look here," Jacob scrolled through a few more pictures, and all had the same signature in the bottom right corner. "So, I started adding to their art," Jacob's voice grew with excitement as he spoke more about it. "I'd add a hat to one of their cat paintings, and then they would add a monocle. We went back and forth for a few months until we started leaving notes hidden under the train. He calls himself 'Railway Diaries' in the letters."

"How did you figure it out? How do you hide your notes, and where do you find theirs? How do you even keep them dry when it rained all afternoon?" Liam asked quickly, without giving Jacob time to answer between questions.

"It took some figuring out, but we have a good system now. We put them in these plastic zipped bags to keep them dry, see?" From the front pocket of his backpack, Jacob pulled a dirty plastic bag and an elastic band, which Liam did not ask but assumed was a way to fasten it to the bottom of the train car.

"But do you know who they are?" Liam asked.

"I don't know anything other than they go to Brookeside High School over in Boulder Ridge," Jacob answered, his voice ringing with a slight reluctance.

"So that's why you come here every day? To hide notes?"

Jacob laughed without humor. "Something like that," he paused momentarily before he continued. "Sometimes, it's nice just to escape it all, you know?

Sometimes, I don't want to do any of this anymore. I just feel like no one understands me or cares to try. At school, at home. But out here, it's easy just to be myself. I don't feel like a nobody," Jacob paused in reflection. "I guess it's probably just because they don't know me."

Liam tried not to show that Jacob's words had an effect on him. To him, he had always looked up to Jacob. Maybe not how all younger brothers look up to their older brothers, but he was proud to be his brother. Liam was glad Drew was not with them to hear Jacob say these things, or he'd probably laugh at him about this, too. Liam watched as Jacob continued walking a few steps ahead of him, and without warning, Liam ran up behind him, grabbed the camera from his hand, and snapped a picture of them together. Liam with a big smile, and although Jacob would not have admitted it, he was half smiling as well.

"Dude, give me my camera back!" Jacob said harshly, but Liam could tell that he was less annoyed than he was trying to appear. Liam gave the camera back to Jacob and was pretty sure that Jacob had quickly deleted the picture.

"There's Drew," Liam pointed to a parking lot as they turned the corner into the mini-mall lot. "I'm sorry that Drew made fun of you, Jacob."

"It's not your fault; you don't have to be sorry. I shouldn't have told Drew about this, anyway. I should have known that he would just make a joke out of it. Drew makes fun of everything."

Together, the two brothers met Drew at his car, grabbed the cans from the backseat, and walked across the parking lot. It was almost dark when the door chimed as the brothers walked into Mr. Lister's Convenience store.

"Well, if it isn't my favorite Robertson trio! How are my favorite delinquents?" Mr. Lister burst into a chuckle straight from his belly, coming around from behind the counter and hugging each of the brothers as they walked through the door.

Mrs. Lister nodded to the brothers from behind the counter, where she was meticulously counting out a roll of dimes into the cash drawer, just to be sure the bank had not missed any. Mrs. Lister was a bookkeeper who knew the cost of everything, even a smile. She was tall and thin, with straight red hair and round, thick-rimmed glasses. Despite her stern appearance, she was kind-hearted, and though she did not do it often, when she did smile, out of practice, her lips would curve and narrow into the corner of a slight dimple, into what could be described as more of a wince than a smile. She was always dressed cleanly and properly.

Almost as different as night and day, Mr. Lister was not very tall, falling a few inches below his wife's height. Despite this, somehow, his shirts would barely cover his entire belly and were often stained with the wear of the day, and his greying hair was always a mess and was well over due for a cutting, in Mrs. Lister's opinion. But despite his messy appearance, Mr. Lister was a very kind man and was most known for his roaring laughs and for always smiling. He liked all the kids that walked through his store doorway, but the three Robertson brothers were particularly special to him.

The brothers stayed just long enough for Mr. Lister to count the cans and give each brother ten dollars.

"Ten dollars? Each?" Mrs. Lister gasped as quietly under her breath as her sudden shock would allow. "Jim, I never!" she continued as she walked into the back room and closed the door loud enough to let her husband know she disapproved.

Mr. Lister did not even acknowledge her as she left the room. "Say hello to your old man for me!" Mr. Lister insisted. "And here's a little something extra," he said as he looked around to make sure that his wife had not walked back into the room. He slipped each boy a chocolate bar. The boys thanked Mr. Lister and promised to come back again soon.

The drive back home was silent, with nothing but the wind through the windows and the engine as it tried to keep up with Drew's foot on the gas pedal making noise. It was evident to Liam that Drew had given up trying to keep up with his one-sided conversation. The three approached the house, walking slowly up the worn sidewalk to the front door, the dried leaves crunching beneath their feet almost loud enough to drown out the sound of Liam's heart beating. His sweaty hand fumbled with the door handle as he quietly tried to turn it. The smell of a cigarette burning away to ash in the tray was the first indication that their father was awake; the sound of him yelling at the TV from his chair was the next.

The boys tried to go upstairs unannounced, but the wind slamming the door as they went to close it gave them away.

"Boys!?" their father yelled, getting up from his dining room table chair with a beer in hand.

The boys waited at the stairs that lead up from the living room until their father stumbled into the kitchen and demanded them into the room. As they walked single file into the kitchen, their father took a few drunk, heavy steps towards them, the floorboards squeaking beneath each stumble. In his mind, Liam returned to the first time he noticed that squeak in the kitchen floorboards. He was eleven years old and had snuck away from his homework and down the stairs to grab a snack when he saw his father wrap his arms around his mother's frail body and pull her in for a dance across the kitchen. By this time, cancer had spread throughout her body, and although the family had tried to remain optimistic about her prognosis, she was a shell of the woman she once was. Once so beautiful and full of life, she now struggled to find the strength just to smile. Even with her deterioration and dinner burning as it was left unattended on the stove, the sound of them laughing and dancing across that squeaky floor was one of Liam's most cherished memories. He did not think back to many of his treasured memories often if he could help it, and now the only time that floor would squeak would be when this man, who never found the bottom of the bottle, would stumble across it.

"Drew?" their father snared. "I was starting to wonder when you'd be gracing us with your presence. How is your exciting life of doing nothing?" He laughed, whistling into the bottle as he took another sip from his beer. He looked down his nose at Drew as he waited for his reaction.

The brothers said nothing as they turned back towards the stairs, hoping that would put an end to the conversation.

"Jacob! Don't turn away from me! I got a call from your principal today about you punching a kid in the face." Their father slurred and spat, "What the hell's the matter with you?"

"He seriously deserved it!" Jacob shouted back.

"I don't care if he half murdered you. You make me look pretty stupid when I get a call like that outta nowhere!"

"Whatever, Dad," Jacob turned to walk back to the stairs but before taking a step he felt a crack at the back of his head. As Jacob fell to the floor. He lay there, cradling his head in his hands. Liam bent to his knees, placing each arm around Jacob's shoulders, trying to help him stand up. Liam felt a burning anger bubbling through his chest but he said nothing as he tried to help Jacob to his feet. After a couple of moments, Jacob stood up slowly, dizzy, taking a moment to regain his footing.

"You're good for nothing, you've always been good for nothing, and you'll always be good for nothing!" their father growled, stepping another step closer to Jacob, who was still struggling to stand straight. Jacob would not let their father see just how much pain he was in—he would not give him the satisfaction. Their father now stood so close to Jacob that as he spoke, the spit out of his mouth was spraying onto Jacob's face.

"Stop it, Dad!" Liam yelled out, taking a big step forward between them, his voice cracking under his panic. He regretted this the exact moment the words left his lips. Liam knew this would only make his father angrier about getting involved, but he could not help it. His heart knocked on his throat as he braced himself for whatever would come next. Without warning, their father raised his hand and slapped Liam. Liam's eyes swelled with tears as he felt his cheek welt. There was a pain in his chest, a deep sadness, almost a hatred. Liam had always tried very hard not to hate his father, but as the years dragged on and the time between the physical fights became shorter, Liam felt as though he was running out of excuses for him.

Jacob took a stumbled step closer and was now pushing back against his father's face, with either a tear from his eye or sweat from his forehead running down his face. His father took a step backward, raising his hand to hit his son again. Drew stepped in between them, pushing Jacob back with his arm, and as he did, their father took a small step backward. Their father's cruel blue eyes were burrowing into Drew, waiting for him to make the next move. This was the first time their father had looked over his oldest son in quite some time. He noticed that Drew's shoulders were now broader than his own and then that his chin had to tilt up to meet Drew's eyes.

Drew and their father stood, holding their stare for a long moment until Drew broke contact and turned back to look at Jacob. "Jacob, just stop!" Drew yelled before turning around again, "Don't bother Dad. He seriously isn't even worth it!"

"You hear that, Jacob? Your own brother agrees you aren't even worth it." He then lifted the bottle to his lips, then poured what was left of it onto Jacob's head until it was empty. "You best be gone before long, Drew, and I don't wanna see you here again. I'll deal with you later, Jacob."

Jacob ran upstairs, slamming the door to his bedroom. Liam walked into his bedroom, and Drew followed him in.

"You still sleep with stuffies on your bed?" Drew laughed, grabbing what was once a fox off Liam's bed.

"It was the last gift Mom ever gave me," Liam said, reaching out for Drew to pass it to him.

Drew tossed it into Liam's hand. "Well, it's been washed so many times it looks like road kill now," Drew laughed again.

Liam sat on his bed, placing his fox on the nightstand beside him, and sat silently.

"You mad at me, Liam?" Drew asked, moving the blanket over the bed and sitting beside Liam.

Liam curled up into the corner of his bed, leaning against the wall, and took a moment before answering. At first, Liam was surprised that Drew would ask him that, as if he had not been part of what happened downstairs. Liam placed his hand on his cheek, which was still hot and had a red hand mark across it. He knew that he was not just mad at Drew, but mad at the world. He felt like he had been cheated. He wondered why they could not be like other families that sat together at the dinner table and went on happy vacations together. He would even settle for being able to be in the same room together.

"I just don't get why you treat Jacob like you do," Liam finally responded.

"Like what?"

"Like you're punishing him, you never stick up for him, especially with Dad."

"He has to learn sometime if he keeps yapping his mouth off, people are going to keep kicking the crap out of him. It's really not my fault he's a slow learner."

Suddenly, Liam heard from across the hall as Jacob opened and slammed his bedroom door, shaking the pictures on Liam's dresser. Liam watched Jacob walk into the bathroom directly across the hallway from his bedroom door, but stood outside Liam's door, pausing for a moment longer than a glance. Jacob flashed a smile at Liam before oddly, gently closing the door behind him.

Thoughts swirled around in Liam's mind as he tried to decipher what the smile meant. Maybe Jacob was thanking him for sticking up for him, or perhaps it was just a sympathetic smile since their father had hit Liam, too. Liam huffed as he looked back to Drew, crossing his arms against his chest, "Well, I don't think it's right. He has a hard enough time without his own brother picking on him, too."

"You're too nice, Liam. That's your problem. You always think life will get better, but it doesn't. You just get smarter."

"I don't agree," argued Liam. "One day, when we all make it out of here, and when we have all made it to the other side of this, we'll look back and realize it's the things we did now that matter. They have to matter."

Drew laughed loudly, covering his mouth to hide his smile, when he realized Liam was not joking. Trying to choke down his laugh with a cough, Drew replied, "You've been spending way too much time with Mr. Lister! I don't think there is any 'making it out of here.' If it isn't our problems

here, it's our problems out there. Life is just one problem after another!" Drew stood up from the bed, looking down at Liam. "You have to grow up sometime, Liam.
You can't always play everything safe. Sometimes things just don't work out."

Liam said nothing, pushing himself further into the corner. Liam wondered how his brother could not spend any time thinking about the future. To Liam, the hope of a better life 'someday' was the only thing that got him through most days. If Liam was not thinking about the future, he was trying hard not to think about the past. Despite all efforts, Liam would find his thoughts wandering to when his mother was alive. To when his father would come home from his shift at the mill, and then everyone would all sit around the table for dinner. Liam had no memory of a time when their mother was not sick or when times were truly good. However, hoping that they were living through what would be the most challenging time of their life and that they all just had to make it through to the other side. Liam did everything he could to hold on to the memories of his past while grasping onto the hope of a better future, and it made Liam feel heavy to look at his brothers, who had no hope for a better future and pushed down all the good memories because of the painful contrasts they made with life now.

Liam was so lost in thought that he did not notice the tear roll down the side of his cheek, but Drew must have seen it and changed his tone. "Listen, if it'll make you feel better, I'll try to apologize to him, or at least try to smooth it over." Drew walked out of Liam's room and across the hallway to the bathroom and knocked on the door, looking across the hall at Liam. "Jacob?" Drew knocked a few more times with no answer. "Jacob?" he called again while he twisted the door handle and tried to open the it, but there was a weight pushing back like something had fallen in front of the door that would not budge. As Drew pushed the door again, he looked down at his feet, feeling the warmth of a pool of blood widening beneath the door.

"Jacob, Jacob, no!" Drew screamed as he tried harder to push the door open, but with all his weight slamming against the door, it would slam back shut with each push. "Liam! Liam! Call 911!"

As quickly as Liam could, he grabbed the phone and dialed 9-1-1.

The call was answered before a second ring. "911 emergencies! Police, fire or ambulance?"

Liam's chest rose and fell with rapid breaths. His pulse raced as those words looped in his mind and back out of his mouth back to Drew, "Police, fire, or ambulance?"

Chapter 4

~The Weight of Absence~

"Hold on, Jacob. Please, just hold on!" Drew's cries echoed off the four walls of the small bathroom, but went unanswered. "Help is coming! Just hold on!"

With Liam's help, Drew was able to push open the bathroom door that Jacob had fallen in front of. Drew lifted Jacob's head, his neck falling limp under his arm, and his eyes stared at the ceiling with a cold, unresponsive gaze; a pool of blood from Jacob's wrist was growing wider around them. Liam felt sick to his stomach, the copper smell filling his airways as he breathed in havoc breaths.

Liam ran downstairs to let the paramedics in when there was a loud knock at the door. They ran upstairs, pealed Jacob from Drew's arms, and swept him away to the hospital. Drew tried to shake their father awake, who was passed out on the couch. Their father never opened his eyes, no matter how hard Drew shook him, and Drew left him there. Drew and Liam rushed behind the ambulance on the rain-washed streets, the red and blue lights piercing through the darkness of the night.

Upon arriving at the hospital, Liam and Drew sat in the waiting room for what felt like a hundred lifetimes, holding onto hope that Jacob would pull through and this would all be behind them soon. Drew tried to wipe his red hands clean onto his shirt, which was already red with blood, only staining his hands more.

Liam heard Drew pull in a deep breath as he stood up and looked at the doctor who was walking towards them, whose head was low and shoulders heavy and had a dreaded look about him. Liam stood up with Drew to meet the doctor, but he did not notice the heaviness in the doctor's demeanor because he was too busy staring at Drew, and a strange look came across his face. Liam was unsure if it was anger, worry, or sadness, but whatever it was, it made Liam feel small and helpless. When the doctor reached them, he told them in the way that only a man who'd shared heartbreaking news a hundred times could, that there was nothing that they could have done to save Jacob's life, and then handed them both a pamphlet about suicide victims' family support. With an open hand on each of their shoulders, he told them he was so sorry for their loss. "If you'd like, we can give you time to say goodbye."

Liam and Drew followed the doctor down the long, bright white hallways. The sounds of machines beeping from every room grabbed Liam's attention as they passed them. Liam felt like his brain was washed clean of everything around him and followed further down the hallway mindlessly. Eventually, they came to a room, where Jacob was lying on a starched white sheet with another sheet pulled up to his chest. His face was pale, and his lips and eyebrows looked almost purple in the room's bright light. Liam felt the need to call out to him when he walked into the room, but he did not. To Liam, he looked like he was just asleep. Liam felt a chilling numbness spread from his fingers across his entire body as he walked inside the room.

"Take all the time you need, boys," the doctor said to them. "Please let us know if you need anything," then he left the room, closing the door behind him.

Liam stood beside the bed, but was not sure what he was supposed to do. The room felt empty, and although Jacob laid on the bed, he felt hollow to look at, as if he was not there at all. Liam looked at Drew, who had sat on a chair next to the bed, holding his head in his hands but not making a sound. Liam walked next to the bed and went to take Jacob's hand in his own, and he gasped and quickly pulled his hand back. Liam had never touched someone whose skin was cold before.

The silence was broken by a gentle knock on the door. "Hi, boys," said a voice as the door slowly opened. "My name is Officer Harlow. I just need to ask you a few questions."

Liam looked at the officer and nodded, his head heavy. Drew's head never left the palms of his hands.

"First of all, we tried calling the number from the hospital records, but there was no answer. Is there anyone we can call to come be with you boys? Your parents or guardians?"

Liam looked at Drew and then slowly back at the officer and shook his head.

"Okay," Officer Harlow continued. "Well, do you boys need a ride home or anything?"

Again, Liam shook his head.

"Well," the officer continued. "Here's my card. I'll be in touch over the next few days for official statements. I've got your address and phone number from the medical files. Meanwhile, if there's anything you need, please call me."

Liam took the card and put it into his pocket. The officer nodded at the two brothers and quietly left the room. Liam could hear the officer mumbling in the hallway to the doctor but could not make out anything that was said, and he did not even care to try to listen.

The two brothers stayed in the room with Jacob for a while. In the silence, neither of them said anything to the other. Drew indicated it was time to leave by standing up and walking to the door. Liam took a moment before following him and looked back at Jacob, trying to make a memory of every part of Jacob's face, knowing this was the last time he'd ever get to see him. Liam closed his eyes as he turned away, hung his head low into his shoulders, and as he opened his eyes again, a tear fell from his lashes, and then he closed the door behind him.

Liam said nothing to Drew on the drive home. Although the silence gave way for his mind to run free, he decided that if the silence was to break, it would be Drew who would break it. Drew said nothing, either. As they walked in the front door, they could see their father still passed out on the couch. Drew had tried to wake him hours before as they were leaving for the hospital, but neither of the brothers cared to try to wake him now.

"I'll spend the night tonight and tell him in the morning," Drew told Liam. "I'm just going to grab some stuff I forgot from the car. I'll be right back."

"Drew?" Liam called. "How do you think this happened?"

"What do you mean?" Drew asked.

"Like, how did Jacob's accident happen?"

Drew looked at Liam, his tired eyes softening as he went to answer, "Jacob took his own life, Liam. He committed suicide."

"No, he wouldn't have!" Liam cried out in shock. "He would never just leave me here without him!"

"Go upstairs, Liam. I'll be right up."

Liam stood for a moment in disbelief. What Drew had said made no sense to him, and it was impossible to believe that Jacob would take his own life and leave him behind. Liam carried these thoughts to the bottom of the stairs, and as he looked up at them, he had to remind himself to breathe. Liam drew in another deep breath as he stepped onto the first step, walking as far as he could to the right side, using the stair rail to brace himself as he walked over the blood stains and bloody footprints that were all over the stairs. Once Liam had gotten into his bed, he laid down, waiting for Drew to come up. His eyes burned as he stared at the ceiling where a tiny bit of light was coming in from the window from the street lights outside. Liam heard as Drew opened the front door, expecting him to come up the stairs right away. Instead, he could hear Drew speaking downstairs.

"Dad must be awake now," he thought as he sat up from his bed, contemplating if he should go downstairs. He wanted to be there for what was left of his fragmented family and find comfort in his father for himself as well. Liam listened from his bed a bit longer and was surprised that his father was not yelling. He could only hear Drew's voice, but it was muffled by his own racing heart. Liam padded across his bedroom floor and opened his door wider as he tried to listen to what Drew was saying. Just as Liam was about to step into the hallway and walk down the stairs, he heard the front door open and slam shut and a glass break, sounding like it had been smashed against the wall. Then he heard his father yell something he could not quite understand. Liam jumped as he heard another glass thrown against the wall. He turned back to his bedroom window when he heard Drew's car roar to a start and then speed up the road.

Liam quietly walked back to his bed and pulled the twisted blanket over his chin; his entire body was sore in a uniformed ache, his eyes burned, his head was pounding, and now he was alone. Liam cried harder than he had ever cried until he had no tears left. He laid in the sound of his labored breathing, trying to steady himself. He could feel the darkness in his bedroom, as if it were surrounding and consuming him. Weakly, he stretched over his bed and turned on the lamp on his bedside table, hoping that having a light on would make him no longer afraid to close his eyes. Liam lay awake for a long while, but eventually, fatigue overtook him, and he passed out from exhaustion,

Liam was jolted awake by the cold air as it was pulled into his window by the front door of the house being opened. The light outside the window indicated that it was sometime in the morning, but he felt like he had just closed his eyes to fall asleep. He sat up quickly, his flush, tear-stained face almost sticking to the pillow as he rose. As Liam rubbed his eyes, the fog of sleep faded, and the realization of all that had happened the night before rushed over him. He laid back in bed, pulling his knees into his body and twisting his blanket back up to his chin. From downstairs, he could hear the murmurs of a conversation coming from the front door. He turned to his bedroom doorway, wanting to listen to who was downstairs. The voices grew louder as they walked from the front door into the living room.

"Want a beer?" Liam heard his father ask.

"No, I'm good, thanks," Liam heard in reply, but was still unsure who it was.

"There won't be a funeral. I've already released the boy's body to the morgue for crem..."

"Your son," the voice interrupted
sternly. "Your son's body. And you have two other sons who
deserve the chance to say a proper goodbye."

"Mr. Lister?" Liam thought to himself, with a warmth
of comfort coming over him.

Liam heard a beer bottle crack open. He waited to
hear his father speak again, but it was silent for a long
moment.

"You know, I've always tried to be a good friend to
you," he was sure now that it was Mr. Lister's voice that he
could hear downstairs as he quietly made his way over to the
doorway to listen better. "I tried to be there for you all
through high school, at your wedding, and I've tried to look
out for your boys since you've been
grieving Susan's passing."

There was another long pause. Still, Liam heard
nothing from his father.

"Now I'd like to check on your boy upstairs since
someone has to," Liam heard Mr. Lister's voice get louder as
he walked towards the stairs. "Maybe you could find it in
yourself to check in on him sometime, too."

Liam returned to bed and waited to hear Mr. Lister walk up the stairs. Still, it sounded like he must have stopped at the bottom, maybe waiting for a response from the living room, or perhaps it was the carpet stained with bloody footprints from the paramedics was the reason that he had not come up the stairs yet. Eventually, Liam could hear each heavy step as Mr. Lister made his way up. Once at the top of the stairs, Mr. Lister gently knocked on Liam's open door before walking in. He seemed surprised to see Liam was already awake as he walked into the room.

"Hi, Liam," Mr. Lister walked over to the bed. Liam sat up again. His puffy eyes looked up at Mr. Lister, and it looked as though he had spent the night crying in his bed and had not slept at all. Liam moved over, allowing room for Mr. Lister to sit on the edge of the bed.

"How are you doing this morning? Do you need anything?" Mr. Lister asked, leaning back on his arm, which was resting on Liam's headboard behind him.

"I'm okay," Liam replied. "I don't think I need anything." The truth was that Liam felt numb. Everything that had happened the night before had felt like a bad dream that he had just woken up from. Still, in the light of the day, it did not feel real. But he knew that it was. He knew that his brother was gone. But he was unsure how he was supposed to feel or what he was supposed to do now. Again, he could feel his eyes swelling with tears as he pushed the blankets off of him, leaned into Mr. Lister's big belly, and then fell into a hug. "We'll never be the *Robertson Trio* again," he cried. "I just don't get it. Why would he do this? Didn't he know how much I loved him?"

Mr. Lister held the boy tightly, his own eyes heavy and wet. "I promise you, this kid, what your brother did had nothing to do with you. He was hurting, but he loved you." The two sat in a hug for a couple more minutes. Mr. Lister could tell that something had caught Liam's attention at the doorway and turned to look. From the bed, he could see straight across the hallway to the bathroom floor, where there was still a mess of Jacob's blood.

Mr. Lister sighed as his head fell, his eyes looking at Liam. "I'm going to clean that up, kid." Standing up from the bed, he walked over and closed the bathroom door, and then he continued, "Why don't you run down to my store while I do? Help yourself to whatever you want. Just let Mrs. Lister know it's on me."

"Thanks, Mr. Lister, but I think I'll go to school."

"Oh gosh, Liam," Mr. Lister's voice sounded heavy with worry. "You don't have to go in today. Given what's happened, I'm sure that the school will understand you taking some time off."

"I know that, but I don't want to just sit here either," he said, getting up from his bed. "I'm going to get ready." Liam went downstairs for a while, leaving Mr. Lister sitting on his bed while brushing his teeth in the kitchen sink, trying to avoid the bathroom.

Liam got dressed and grabbed his backpack from his bedroom floor.

"Well, be sure to bring a jacket. The wind is a bit cold out there this morning,"

Liam looked around for his coat, catching a glimpse of it hanging on Jacob's bedroom door. He remembered that he had let Jacob wear it the day before. Liam stepped inside just far enough to grab the coat from the door handle and be out but spotted Jacob's camera sitting on his dresser. He grabbed it, put it into his backpack, and after saying goodbye to Mr. Lister, walked downstairs, out the door, and was off to school.

The walk to school was short, and within half an hour, he was walking up the sidewalk to the front entrance. As he passed other students walking towards the school, it did not take Liam long to realize that word does travel fast in a small town. He felt everyone looking at him, or heard them whispering about him. Liam had reached the school and walked up the grass to the steps. As he walked up the front steps, he paused momentarily with his hand on the front door before opening it. The hallway was bustling with busy kids on their way to their first classes, but the hall fell silent as they looked at the door as it opened and then closed. Everyone stood in place, their hungry eyes devouring Liam as he walked to his locker. There was nowhere for him to look without his eyes getting caught up in someone else's, so Liam stared down at the floor as he walked. Everyone looking at him made Liam's face flash crimson. He would have left the moment he walked in if he had anywhere other than home to go. The hallways quickly returned to its busy state, as the students rushed here and there.

"Liam!" Nick called over, "I really didn't think you'd be here today,"

Liam said nothing. The two just stood in the center of the busy hallway. It was clear to Liam that Nick did not know what to say, but Liam did not mind. Liam did not know what to say to Nick either. There was no way to put his own feelings into words, so he did not expect Nick to. The sound of the school bell ringing ended their exchange. Liam walked to his class, feeling guilty that he did not even know how to talk with his best friend, and had made the entire thing more awkward than any conversation had ever been between them.

Liam was the last to arrive in his first class, and there were still a few minutes before class was to start. The students were all conversing, but as soon as Liam walked in, the entire room fell so quiet that they could hear the chatter from the class across the hallway. Liam walked as quickly as he could to his desk without looking at anyone and sat down. The classroom was filled with chatter again until someone that no one recognized walked into the room and stood at the front of the room at the teacher's desk.

"Hello, class. My name is Ms. Walsh," the unfamiliar voice said from the front of the room, calling the class to order. "I will be substituting for Mr. Doyle's science class today. Please take out your lessons from yesterday; we'll pick up where you left off."

Liam stared at the clock at the front of the desk, unaware of what was happening around him. As Ms. Walsh walked to the office to turn in her attendance, most of the class kids whispered and nodded in Liam's direction. Liam was too distracted, now looking out the window, to notice. His chin resting on the palm of his hand as he stared at nothing in particular outside. His tired eyes felt like puffed-up pillows, and so he laid his head on his desk.

In the back corner of the classroom sat Alex Jones. Liam had known Alex since the third grade, when he was sent home at least once a week for burning ants with a magnifying glass during recess, nearly burning down the playground field a few times. Now, Alex did not necessarily pick on Liam more than he did any other student. He was still the same kid he was in the third grade, but now the entire class was his ant hill. With Ms. Walsh away, Alex was ripping off the corners of his paper and was spitting spitballs at the back of Liam's head. Liam could barely muster the energy to lift his head off his folded arms on his desk, let alone turn and ask Alex to stop. He sat there, staring out the window, his eyes burning like they had been washed with sandpaper.

"Leave him alone, Alex!" Shouted Suzanne, the girl sitting in front of Liam. Suzanne was class president and president of the chess club and always tried to talk the teachers into assigning homework. She was always the first to raise her hand to answer any question in class and always sat in the front row. But most of all, Suzanne was always there to remind the class and even the teachers of any and all the rules, even when the teacher was out of class and could not see her. She did not play by the book; she lived by the book.

"Who are you, his mom?" Alex laughed to a few other boys around him before pressing his lips against the plastic straw and spitting another, landing it on the back of Liam's chair.

Suzanne glared at Alex as she walked around her desk and over to Liam, perching herself over his desk. "Do you want me to go get the teacher?"

Liam shook his head.

Suzanne stood for a moment; the left side of her face curled down into a frown. "Well, I just wanted to say that I'm sorry for what happened to your brother Liam."

"Thank you," Liam responded, unsure if that was the proper response.

Suzanne turned around and sat back at her desk, shooting another glare in Alex's direction.

Just as Alex had loaded and spat another spitball at the back of Liam's head, Ms. Walsh walked into the classroom, "you! With the straw in your teeth, go to the principal's office immediately!" she scolded, pointing her long finger at the door.

Alex huffed, scraping his chair in a long, intentional scrape across the floor as he stood up and kicked Liam's foot as he walked by.

"Come up here…" Ms. Walsh said, staring at Liam, waiting for him to respond.

"Liam," he answered as he walked to the front of the classroom.

"Liam, I can't help but notice that you have not even opened your lesson. I know that bullying is a big deal, but you still have an obligation to complete your work in my class. If you don't, I will have to send you to the principal's office as well. Do you understand me?"

Liam nodded and returned to his desk, passing Suzanne, who looked at him like he was a lost puppy dog. Liam sat down, looking at his paper with his pencil in hand. Although he did not complete a single question, to Ms. Walsh, at least it looked like he spent his time working on his lesson.

The class bell rang, and Liam was the first out the door. Liam was walking with his head down to his locker when a loud voice came over the announcer, "*All students, please head to the gym for a mandatory assembly.*"

Liam walked down the hallway to the gym and was thankful to see Nick outside the gym doors, waiting for him. Together, the two walked in. All the students were seated in the bleachers, and in front of them were Principal Johnson and the school counselor, Mr. Wydler.

"We have invited a grief counselor, Mrs. Kelly, here to speak to you all," Mr. Wydler said, his open palm in the direction of a smartly dressed, tall woman sitting on the first bleacher, "She has come to talk to you all about the feelings you might all be going through today and the effect of suicide has on a tight-knit school like ours. Mrs. Kelly, if you would."

Liam looked around to see that everyone was staring at him again. He pulled his hood to cover his face and leaned forward. Mrs. Kelly walked up and stood next to Mr. Wydler, thanking him, and then addressed the students.

"Mr. Wydler has called me in to talk to you about losing one of your fellow classmates, Jacob. The effects of such a loss can be felt by everyone, and I know Mr. Wydler has had several students that were close with Jacob come to him about how to handle their own grief over his loss."

Liam scoffed to himself. It was hard to believe that any of these kids were close enough to feel his loss. He looked around to see the same kids who had made every day at school a nightmare for Jacob, now crying to each other. Some were just hushed whispers expressing their sadness. Others wiped tears from their stone-dry eyes. Liam wondered how all of these kids could put on such an act now when they had never even been bothered to notice his brother before, and those who did were not kind. Anger simmered beneath the surface of Liam's grief, a bitter resentment towards all those who sought to claim a connection to his loss. This was Liam's brother, and as he sat silently in his seat, staring at Mrs. Kelly, his mind was miles away, and an emptiness echoed in his heart.

Before he knew it, the rest of the students were standing up and walking out of the gym. Liam followed behind Nick, who told him that he would see him later and left to grab the books for his next class. As Liam was about to pass Jacob's locker, he noticed it was covered in blue, yellow, and pink sticky notes full of 'sincere condolences,' and flowers surrounding the floor around it. Liam walked closer to have a look when he felt two hands on his back, pushing him hard, his face smashing into the locker next to Jacob's.

Liam spun around to see Alex Jones in front of him. His face was red hot with anger, and he glared and shouted at Liam. "You got me a call home!"

"I didn't do anything," Liam responded, rubbing his hand against his sore jaw.

"You think you get to play the sympathy card just because your brother decided to kill himself? I'm still going to beat the crap outta you for getting me in trouble. After you get outta school, you and me," Alex's mouth curled into a smile that almost looked carved into his freckled cheeks, "your big brother isn't here anymore to protect you. Besides, did he commit suicide, or was he just dying for attention?" Alex laughed, "Or maybe he just got sick of having a brother like you and decided to take the easy way out."

Now Liam felt hot with rage. He could feel it bubbling up from his stomach, and in a split second, he jumped at Alex, knocking him to the ground. Liam sat on Alex's chest, punching him once hard in the face. Liam's eyes opened wide as he looked at Alex's face, which quickly flashed with fear before he raised his hands to cover himself. Liam's hand felt as though it was tied in a knot as it crumpled to his side. His stomach felt tied in knots, too.

"I'm sorry, I'm sorry!" Liam scrambled off of Alex and to his feet, "I'm so sorry!"

Alex was back on his feet in a hurry, grabbing Liam by the front of his sweater and lifting him against the locker. "You're going to be sorry!" Alex hissed at Liam, striking his fist in Liam's gut. Liam buckled onto the floor, holding his stomach, trying to catch his breath after all the air had been knocked out of him. Alex lifted Liam to his feet, but just as Alex was about to land another punch into Liam, someone grabbed Alex's shoulders from behind, pulling him back and away from Liam.

Standing in front of Liam and Alex was Steven Farlow. His bruised black eye from the fight with Jacob the day before seemed darker than it naturally should as he glared at Alex, stepping between the two of them. Alex stared at Steven for a moment, waiting for him to back down, but then Alex grabbed his own backpack from the floor and walked away, flashing an angry glare at Liam as he pushed past him.

Steven ensured Alex was around a corner before he turned to Liam, whose head was looking down at his feet, and his arm was still pulled against his stomach. Steven looked at Liam; both were silent for a long moment before Steven finally spoke, "I'm really sorry about your brother, Liam."

Liam looked up at Steven but said nothing. Then Liam quickly walked away, pushing past the other kids that had gathered around, he ran down the hall and into the bathroom, locking himself in an empty stall. Liam felt sick, but he was not sure if he was going to puke or cry, or both. Liam sat on the toilet in a stall, lifting his feet off the floor to hide as other kids entered the bathroom.

"I've never seen Liam act like that before. He must just be mad about his brother dying," said one kid.

"I think he's probably just trying to be like Jacob now that he's gone. Why else would he suddenly start fighting? It just seems weird," said another.

These words were in Liam's head like marbles, and it took him another ten minutes to compose himself after all the other kids had left the bathroom and enough to come out of the stall. He looked at himself in the mirror with disgust as he walked to the door and out of the bathroom. Liam looked both ways down the hallway to be sure the crowds of kids had made their way to their classes.

"Maybe Mr. Lister was right," Liam thought, deciding to go home and hide away in his room for the day.

As Liam walked past Mr. Doyle's science class, catching Ms. Walsh's attention, she quickly came to the doorway, calling down the hallway after him. He turned to her, flashing a quick smile, trying to hide that he still had tears in his eyes.

"Liam!" she called to him again. He walked over to the classroom door, which she had now closed, and she was now tapping her foot as she waited for him to walk over. Ms. Walsh placed her hand on Liam's shoulder, and although he knew she was trying to comfort him, her hand was ice cold on his shoulder, compelling him to take a step back. Ms. Walsh matched his step but pulled her hand back by her side. "Suzanne told me about your brother, and I just wanted to say that I'm so sorry. I hope that you didn't feel I was trying to embarrass you in front of the classroom; I didn't know."

"It's okay, Ms. Walsh." Liam hung his head on his shoulders, mustering as much of a smile as he could and continuing down the hallway.

Liam walked by the front office, where Principal Johnson and Mr. Wydler were talking with what seemed like a couple of angry parents.

"I'm not sure why you had to talk to our kids about suicide without our permission?" Liam heard one say, "We have the right to say what our children are exposed to!" said another.

Mr. Wydler spoke up, trying to calm them down, "We felt that given the circumstances, we needed to react quickly, and this needed to be done in order to support the kids in our school who are struggling."

Liam continued walking faster after he saw that Mr. Wydler had seen him walking by and was sure he would want to sit down and *"check in"* with him. Liam turned a corner in the hallway, sure that he could slow down now that he knew that Mr. Wydler was not behind him.

Just as Liam slowed down his pace, he heard his name called. "Mr. Robertson!" the voice boomed from behind him. Liam thought it must be Mr. Wydler, but it did not sound like him. Slowly, Liam turned around towards the voice. It was not Mr. Wydler and Liam had turned around to see the only person he had hoped not to have to talk to today.

Chapter 5

~Echoes of Loss~

Liam walked hesitantly towards Principal Johnson, who was jerking his head towards an open door, looking impatient as he waited for Liam to walk into the office. Liam was steps away from the office when a door between them opened.

"Hello, Principal Johnson," said Mr. Wydler, the school counselor, as he walked through the door between them. "I'd like to speak with Liam now."

"That is not necessary," Principal Johnson insisted, opening the door to his office even wider. "I've gotten a complaint about his behavior, and I'll deal with him in my office!"

"Given the circumstances," Mr. Wydler interrupted, "I think it's best if I spoke with him, but I'll let you know if I need any support in the conversation," Mr. Wydler did not wait for any more argument from Principal Johnson, he walked over to Liam. Although Liam did not overly want to go with Mr. Wydler either, he rushed inside the open door to his office, knowing that it was better than the alternative. Mr. Wydler walked inside and closed the door behind himself. Liam caught a glimpse of Principal Johnson through the doorway, letting out a huff as he stood alone before stomping back into his office.

Walking into Mr. Wydler's office was like walking into a different world from the rest of the school, with its new paint on the walls and carpeted floor. Then again, compared to everyone else who worked at the school, Mr. Wydler himself seemed to be from another world. Everyone knew that Mr. Wydler could have made a lot more money working at a more prestigious school, but here he was, doing what he could. His office was warm, too warm. It was at least two degrees warmer than the rest of the school, which did not feel good against Liam's hot, tear-flushed face.

Liam fell deep into the leather bucket chair across the desk from where Mr. Wydler went to sit after closing the door. Liam scanned the room, looking for anything to keep from meeting Mr. Wydler's eyes that he could feel looking at him. Behind the desk was a bookshelf filled with every self-help book ever written. On the wall to Liam's right were framed diplomas, a life's achievements, hanging in a perfect row without even a speck of dust on them. The smell of lavender from the oil diffuser on the desk drifted into Liam's nose, mixed with the smell of dirt from the freshly watered plants beside him, next to the only window in the small room. The window curtains were drawn closed, and a lamp next to the desk was the only light on. On the desk next to a picture of Mr. Wydler with a woman and a small boy, Liam could hear the steady flow of the water fountain on the desktop. On the other side was a basket full of neatly organized folders.

Mr. Wydler sat down, leaning over his desk in Liam's direction. "I know how it feels to feel out of place, Liam. Growing up, I was one of only a few black kids in my school. To say that I got bullied a lot would be an understatement."

Liam looked at Mr. Wydler. Not at his eyes but at his clothes, noticing that Mr. Wydler was the only man he had ever seen wearing purple. Liam wondered why he had never noticed before or why he was even noticing it now. On this particular day, he wore a dark purple dress shirt and black dress pants, and Liam was sure that if he could see his shoes under the desk, he would notice that they were black and perfectly shined. Mr. Wydler was now fidgeting with the top button, holding his shirt closed, exposing his nerves. Liam was not used to people being nervous around him. In fact, most people just ignored him. But on this day, Liam noticed that everyone seemed nervous around him and did not like how that felt. Like he was now under pressure to make others feel comfortable when he was unsure of how he was supposed to feel himself.

"We didn't expect you to come in today, Liam."

Liam looked down at his hand, pulling on the sleeve of his sweater. "I didn't know where else to go."

Mr. Wydler's face softened, his eyes closing momentarily in sympathy, "Please know that I'm not here to give you trouble about punching Alex. You've never caused any trouble before, and from what I've heard from Ms.

Walsh, it was not unprovoked," Mr. Wydler paused, standing to grab a glass of water from the water dispenser and offering it to Liam. The glass sat before Liam on the desk. Drops of condensation formed around the glass of cold water from the room's warm air. Liam watched as the droplets began to race down the glass onto the hardwood desk.

"Do you want me to use a coaster?" Liam asked.

Mr. Wydler smiled but said nothing as he placed a coaster under Liam's glass and sat back down. "We didn't expect you to be in today, given the circumstances, but I wanted to call you into my office and check in with you."

"Thanks," Liam said, his voice sounding unintentionally reluctant.

"I want you to know how sorry we all are about what happened to your brother," Mr. Wydler said, with all the same sincerity in his voice that Liam had heard from everyone else that day.

"Everyone is sorry," Liam muttered, running his fingers down the outside of the cold, wet glass.

Mr. Wydler clicked his tongue and leaned back into his chair. "It's okay to be mad, Liam."

"I'm not mad!" Liam shouted before coiling back in his chair. "I'm sorry. I didn't mean to yell, but I'm not mad!"

Mr. Wydler's voice softened as he leaned back closer across the desk. "Anger is almost always a secondary emotion, Liam. You're right; you probably aren't mad. Or you probably are not *just* mad. You probably have a range of emotions: sad, hurt, confused. And all of that is okay.

"I am feeling all of that, I guess," Liam said, opening up but trying to sink deeper into the chair's leather.

"Well, it helps to unpack it all one at a time," Mr. Wydler said. "Let's start with why you might be feeling confused."

"I just don't get it, everyone telling me how 'they're so sorry' to me. Jacob's locker is set up like some shrine. But where were all of these people while my brother was still here? Why wasn't anyone sorry then?" Liam wiped a tear before it fell from his eye. "It's just not fair."

"No, it is not fair, Liam." Mr. Wydler smiled in sympathy. "People always look back, wondering what they should have done differently. I'm sure their apologies are genuine, but unless it's something someone has gone through themselves, they really can't understand what you're going through."

Liam looked up at Mr. Wydler, whose face suggested *he* could understand what Liam was going through.

"But none of these people even knew my brother, and those who say they did, never cared enough to make sure he was okay. They're all lined up to say how sorry they are now like it'll make any difference, but where were they when he needed them? Where was everyone when Jacob needed them? "Liam paused, "where was *I*?" Liam's voice weakened as he continued, not wanting to say more, but could not keep the words from pouring out of his mouth. "I just don't get why. Why would he do this? I would have done anything to help him. I would have been anything he needed; he didn't have to do this. We could have run away. I would have carried him if I had to. He didn't have to do this. I just wish I had told him," Liam cried, not even bothering to wipe the tears falling down his cheeks. "But he's gone; he left me here knowing I couldn't follow him; he just left me here!"

"This wasn't your fault, Liam."

"Everyone keeps saying that, but how do I convince myself of that?"

"I know that you probably aren't ready to talk about it all today, but I would like for us to set up meetings to speak once a week," said Mr. Wydler as he got up and turned to the bookshelf behind him. "This is a good book; I recommend you read through it. I do believe it will really help you; I know it helped me."

"*True Loss*," Liam read aloud, "*Navigating Through Hard Times*. Thanks," he said, tapping the book three times with his pointer finger while getting up from the chair and walking towards the door.

"You can stay if you'd like to, Liam," Mr. Wydler offered.

Liam turned back and smiled, then opened the door to the hallway.

"I'll be seeing you soon, Liam. If there's anything you need, please don't hesitate to ask."

Liam walked out of Mr. Wydler's office, down the hallway, and out the front door.

Liam walked at a slower than usual pace, his hands buried into his jeans pocket, and was kicking leaves up on the side walk as he went. Even in the brisk air, Liam's face was burning hot, and the gentle wind stirring around stung his tear-stained face like pins. He pulled his hood over his head to shield himself from the wind when suddenly, he felt his stomach twist into knots as something ahead caught his eye. A block ahead of him was someone standing beside a bike. The rider wore a blue jacket and a hood covering some of his face, but there was something familiar about him. "Jacob?" Liam whispered to himself, "Jacob!" he shouted out loud, picking up his pace until he was running towards him. Liam caught up to the bike rider as he lifted his foot to ride off. "Jacob!" Liam shouted again. The bike rider stopped and looked back, now just a few steps in front of him. The kid pulled down his hood and pulled off the headphones he had covering his ears.

"What's your problem, man?" the stranger asked as he turned to Liam, pausing momentarily to allow him to respond.

"I-I'm sorry," Liam said, taking a few steps backward before turning around and walking back to the sidewalk.

Behind him, Liam could hear the kid pushing off, peddling away.

Liam felt like the world was spinning, and he was standing completely still. He could see people talking on cell phones, friends walking their dogs, and laughing in light conversation.

"How can they all just carry on? Do they not even know?" Liam thought to himself. The world was now different, and he felt he was the only one who could feel it. He wished the world would shrink around him and allow him time to catch up. "How can all of these people just carry on? How could life possibly just carry on? Jacob is dead, and somehow, all these people are just carrying on."

Liam stood at the crosswalk, his chest tight and shoulders heavy. Instead of turning left to go home, he turned right and went down the road that led him to the outskirts of town until he was at the entrance of the mill. Liam ran as fast as he could to the tracks. The mud from the day before had dried, leaving Jacob's footprints hardened like fossils along the side of the tracks. Liam lost all the strength in his legs, falling to his knees. He traced the shoe imprint with his fingers as the tears that had been clinging to his lashes fell down his face. "Just take me back to yesterday!" he yelled, muffling his voice into the sleeves of his sweater. "Just one day, I'll never ask for anything again! Please. I'd never let this happen," he cried, yelling to no one, to everyone. "I'm so sorry, Jacob. I'm sorry I didn't listen to you when you were hurting. I'm sorry that I stood by while Dad hit you, while this all happened to you. I'm sorry, I'm just so sorry." Liam cried, hugging his knees into his chest and burying his eyes into his knees.

Liam cried until he felt that he was out of tears. He sat kneeling for some time, out of tears and had exhausted himself. He had half a mind to lie down and sleep on the side of the train tracks. He just stayed, kneeling, staring at the footprints in the dried dirt. After some time, Liam collected himself enough that he felt the strength to stand, and as he placed his hand on his knee, he felt something crimp in his jacket pocket. Liam dried his tears off his hands and pulled from his pocket an envelope that read, in a distinctive and familiarly messy writing, '*From Jacob.*'

Liam stared at the envelope for a moment. His eyes widened as the realization set in. "This must be Jacob's reply to the letter he got yesterday! He just never got the chance to send it." Liam felt his heart and stomach twist into a ball and they pin-ponged around his upper body.

Liam held the envelope to his chest. Suddenly, and with perfect clarity, Liam realized what he must do. It bubbled up in him, a mix of excitement and nerves. "I am going to get this letter to Railway Diaries myself. I'm going to finish this for Jacob." Liam thought to himself as if deciding that if he could somehow get this letter to the stranger, it would be like saying the goodbye to Jacob that he never got the chance to. Liam did not even wait to figure out exactly how he would do this and ran the entire way home without stopping.

Running around his street corner, Liam stopped abruptly, seeing Drew's car parked beside the driveway where Mr. Lister had been parked earlier. Liam walked down the rest of the street, up the steps, and opened the door quietly. The smell of the cigarette smoke-filled house mixed with the smell of bleach hit Liam's nose and fell to his empty stomach like a bag of bricks. Liam walked as quietly as he could. He looked into the living room, where his father was asleep in his chair. He continued quietly to the stairs. Looking up from the bottom step, he could see Drew sitting at the top.

"Did Mr. Lister leave? He was here earlier, cleaning up."

"Yeah, I saw him. The stairs are dry now," Drew answered. "He told me you went to school. You're home a few hours early. Did the day not go well?"

Liam did not really want to go over how his day went, not with Drew, not with anyone. He wanted to put the day behind him. Liam walked up the stairs and sat on the top step. "No, my day didn't go well, but…"

"But what?" Drew sighed, rubbing his palms across his forehead and through his hair.

Liam did not tell Drew how his day had gone but spent the next few minutes telling him about the envelope he found in his jacket pocket. He spoke slowly, trying not to sound too excited so Drew would take him seriously.

"So what? You found a letter. Open it and see what it says," Drew said, reaching to take it from him.

"No," Liam pulled away, "this letter must be for his pen pal that he told us about yesterday. Railway Diaries is what he called him."

"So what? Jacob didn't bother to get it to him." Drew said, his hand still out for the envelope.

"I'm going to."

Drew sighed intentionally loud. "You're going to what, Liam? How are you going to get this envelope to someone you've never even met? Are you just going to put it on the next train?" He said sarcastically.

"No," Liam answered, leaning eagerly toward Drew. "I want to tell this pen pal what happened to Jacob so the letters don't stop altogether with no answers. I have to do this for Jacob."

Liam's voice shrunk as he noticed that Drew was laughing at him.

"Why are you laughing?" Liam asked; the excitement in his voice had been displaced by disappointment.

"What are you talking about, Liam? Jacob didn't even know who this guy was; what makes you think you'll find him?"

"Jacob told me he goes to Brookeside High School in Boulder Ridge," Liam looked at Drew's face, which was still twisted into a half smile. Not a happy-looking smile, he smiled at Liam in a way that Liam knew meant that he was making fun of him or, at the very least, not taking what he was saying seriously. "I figured I'd just start there. Don't you understand? I have to do this."

"No. I don't get it, Liam," Drew snapped, as his smile vanished. "Did you actually think I was just going to let you go there alone, Liam? It's a four-hour drive away, and I don't think you're even thinking clearly," Drew leaned closer to Liam, "this is not what I meant when I told you that you needed to be braver. The line between brave and stupid is small, but it isn't that thin. This isn't brave; it's just stupid. What are you going to do, walk?"

"I don't want to go alone. I'm asking you to come with me! I know you think this is stupid, but this is important to me. Please, Drew, I'm asking you to come with me," Liam pleaded.

"Come with you to find some guy you don't know what he looks like or his name, so you can give him an envelope that you found? You'd have better luck getting there by train than having me drive you," Drew laughed again. "So, forget it. You're not going."

Liam's face flashed red as he stood up, pushing past Drew, who was still sitting on the top stair.

"I'm sorry, Liam. You'll see that I'm right when you start thinking clearly."

Liam turned to Drew before closing his bedroom door. "You know what? You always do this. You did this to Jacob, and you always do this to me. You think that because you're older, you can just laugh in our faces at anything that's important to us and dictate what we should do or how we should feel. Well, I'm done with it."

"Would you just stop it? Why are you shouting at me?" Drew yelled back, his voice growing increasingly angry as he continued. "Jacob's gone, Liam. He's gone, and this won't bring him back either. Now, just get in your room and forget this stupid idea."

Liam slammed his bedroom door and waited for Drew to leave for the night. He became more and more frustrated as the hour of the clock went by, and Drew had still not left. He lay in his bed, wearing a complete set of clothes down to his socks and an old pair of gym shoes, waiting to hear the roar of Ol' Rusty's engine. Liam waited so long that he thought Drew would never leave, and it was almost three AM when Drew finally got into his car and drove away. Before he had even gone around the corner, Liam grabbed his backpack that he had spent his time equipping with all the cash he had saved from the pop can money, a couple changes of clothes, Jacob's camera, and the envelope safely tucked away in the front pocket. He canvased out his bedroom window. He had never needed to make an escape through it before, but he had seen Jacob and Drew sneak out of the house enough throughout the years that he figured he could figure it out. First, Liam lowered himself from his bedroom window onto an aging shed that was a straight fall from his windowsill, then jumped to the ground below.

"Well, that wasn't half as hard as I thought it was going to be!" He thought to himself, feeling quite accomplished at how his adventure had gone so far. He looked both ways and crossed the road, his shadow leading him under the street lights.

The early morning hours were still dark as Liam walked to the mill yard. The town this time of the night felt strange, but he took comfort in knowing that after he had walked a few blocks from his home, he had reached the more affluent neighborhood, known to the kids of Larsen Creek as 'Snob Street.' It was a newer development of cookie-cutter houses, all spaced perfectly apart and lined with actual white picket fences. The developer had sold them as the '*Real American Dream.*' Just up the street from him, Liam could see someone walking with a dog leash in his hand. At first, Liam was nervous about meeting this approaching man on the empty sidewalk, but as he got closer, he recognized the walker as Mr. Bennett, the local grocery store owner whom Liam knew well. "*What is Mr. Bennet doing walking his dog at three am?*" Liam tried to pass him unnoticed, his face sunk low into his shoulders, looking at his feet.

"You look all packed up like you're running away!" Mr. Bennet laughed, pulling on his dog's leash to get him to stop walking and then instructing him to sit at his feet. Liam nodded with a laugh, trying not to show his face. "Where are you off to, Liam?"

Liam turned towards Mr. Bennet, knowing there was no point in hiding his face since he had already figured out who he was. "Hey, Mr. B, I'm just on my way to my… job!"

"Your job?"

"Yeah, my job. My job at the… paper route," Liam lied. Liam did not like to lie, which is probably why he was not very good at it. Even now, he did not like the sting it left on his tongue after he had said it. But he decided that once he was done what he had to do and delivered the envelope to its rightful owner, he would be sure to apologize to Mr. Bennet. "What about you?" Liam asked, quickly trying to change the subject.

"You're heading to your job, at the paper route, at three in the morning on a school day?" Mr. Bennet's voice held all the expected suspicion.

"Yeah, those papers don't throw themselves! I'd better go now. I don't want to be late! Take care, Mr. Bennet!" Liam's lies stung his tongue again. He grew more anxious as he walked away, waving to Mr. Bennet, breathing heavily through his fake smile as he walked down the sidewalk and turned the corner, and scurried out of sight.

It was a short walk to the mill yard, and thankfully, Mr. Bennet was Liam's only run-in. The mill yard was well lit, too well lit for a boy who planned to hide away on a train car through the night to the next town. Walking carefully along the row of train cars, Liam searched for a place to hide. He found a train car with a ladder, a small landing, and a walkway that Liam could sit safely on, sheltered between it and a railing. It could have been better hidden, but he figured if no one was looking for him, no one would find him. Just as he got settled in, Liam looked to the mill entrance to see if the train looked ready to move. But past the office at the front gate, he could see the lights of Drew's car pull up and heard the squeal of his door opening and closing again.

"Liam!" Drew called as he walked closer, looking for Liam in each train car as he passed by, "I was joking about you taking a train! This isn't just stupid; it's dangerous!"

Liam lay silently, trying to steady his heavy breathing. He could hear Drew's footsteps as he walked closer to where Liam was hidden on the train car, until they abruptly stopped. Liam heard the office door open and then close and a heavy-set man in jeans, a plaid shirt, and a red baseball cap was walking towards the front of the train. Liam tried to listen for Drew but could only hear the man as he walked onto the train and started the engine. The car that Liam had chosen was a long way down from the front, but the train engine still raddled through Liam's chest. Just as he was bracing himself for the train to begin moving, he felt a tight grip on his shoulder as it dragged him off the train and threw him onto the ground.

Liam stood up, but a heavy hand on his shoulder began dragging him towards the front gate. Liam freed himself, and he turned around to see Drew, his face hidden in the shadows cast by the mill lights behind him. The two watched as the train cars slowly passed by them.

"Why are you doing this? Please, just let me do this!" Liam yelled, "You always try to tell me how I'm feeling, or how I should be feeling, or what I can or can't do! I'm going, and you're not going to stop me!"

"It has nothing to do with how you're feeling, Liam!" Drew shouted, the train pressing against the tracks loudly beside them. "It's about keeping you safe!"

"Keeping me safe?" Liam shouted, "You're the one who's always telling me that I play everything too safe. Go away. I don't need you to keep me safe!"

Drew tried to grab Liam again as he ran away, but he could not, and Liam jumped onto the moving train car that was just starting to pick up speed. Drew tried to run after him, but he stopped after a few cars had passed, and he watched the train screech down the railway like tortured metal as it chugged away.

Chapter 6

~Railway Departure~

The train crashed through the darkness, echoing into the deep night. Liam sat, resting against the cold metal walkway. He felt his heart rattling in his chest cavity, his ears and nose numb from the cold, and the cold air like pins and needles against his fingers and cheeks. There was nothing to do to pass the time but to watch the shadows of the trees as they danced in the moonlight beside the tracks as the train sped by them. He pulled his nose into the brim of his coat, the zipper stinging against his bare skin. Liam's ice fingers could hardly bend as he tried to ball them up, shoving them deep into his coat pockets.

Suddenly, as most terrible thoughts come, Liam had a horrible idea, "What if this train was not even bound for Boulder Ridge and I have made a mistake? Maybe there was a change in the train schedule, and now I'll have to find a phone to call Drew to pick me up in some unknown, foreign town far away from home where the train does finally stop. Ugh, and Drew, Drew would drive me home, and I'd have to listen to all his 'I told you so's.' His nerves tinged, threatening to steal all his motivation in what he was doing.

Liam sat with these thoughts for a moment before deciding to shrug them off, remembering something that his mother used to say to him: "*Things always work out, and even if things are going bad, stressing doesn't change anything.*"

Liam put the terrible thought away- for now. The lids of his eyes felt heavy, and despite his muscles tensing as he shivered and his breath fogging into a cloud as it frosted his eyelashes, Liam closed his eyes and allowed the loud humming from the train to lull him into a restless sleep. Liam did not rest much, waking up often, and the feeling of free falling caused him to jerk awake, all his senses forgetting where he was for a moment each time. Liam closed his eyes again, drifting off once more until he was jolted awake enough that he could not fall back asleep, even when he tried to. Liam sat up, reaching into his backpack tucked beside him, and grabbed the camera. He looked through the pictures and paused on the last photo of himself and Jacob, smiling while tears formed, burning in his sandpapered eyes. Liam looked through all the images on Jacob's camera, feeling reassured in his pursuits.

Liam laid his back against the cold metal of the train car; his mind drifted to what Drew was doing. He wondered if Drew had returned to the house and told their father that he had run away and if the two had decided to call the police, who would then be waiting for him in Boulder Ridge. He wondered if his mission was over before it had really begun.

"He's probably already on the way to Boulder Ridge." Liam's negative thoughts wandered again, wishing that he had never mentioned anything to him about where he was going. Liam felt a dread in his chest that was getting heavier and kept feeling like the fight with Drew was irreparable. His thoughts drifted without control, and although he spent a lot of time throughout his life trying not to think about how close he and Drew once were growing up, in the darkness of the night, he found his thoughts carried him away to happier times.

Liam thought back to his favorite memory of Drew, which happened when he was eleven years old. Their father was in a particularly memorable drunken rage, yelling at the three boys over a lost TV remote. Drew brought his two younger brothers upstairs and closed the bedroom door, where he began talking to them about all the facts he knew about the planets. To the average observer, it would just look like an older brother talking to his two brothers about the solar system, but forged into Liam's memory was his older brother protecting him, saving him, and laughing with him. They laughed late into the night over their father's yells below. Liam swallowed over the ball in his throat, his chest tightening as it always did when he thought back on his life. Liam pleaded with himself to think of anything besides the ghosts of a life long gone now.

Liam sat up and saw the glow of city lights in the distance. His back and legs lay stiff as he looked at the approaching town as though it was quietly sleeping in the early morning haze. It had been hours since Liam had left, and now, as he was quickly approaching the town ahead, he brought back all the importance of his mission, and he was now one step closer to delivering the envelope. The brakes began shaking and hissing as the train slowed down as it entered the city limits, the horn bellowing through the quiet city. Liam could now see the street lights come to form as they passed over him, nearly blinding him with their brightness after a long night in the dark. He listened to the boom of the train whistling as it approached the city street.

Liam waited in place, still sitting against the railing, waiting for the train to slow down to a stop as it entered the mill that he had expected to stop at. He watched as the mill passed, with no sign of the train stopping. He wondered where else the train might go in town until he read a sign: 'Now Leaving Boulder Ridge, please come again.' The train passed by without stopping, now picking up speed as it left the town. A sudden rush came over all of Liam's senses at the same time when he realized that the train was not stopping in Boulder Ridge at all.

As the train reached the end of the city limits, it began to pick up speed again, leaving Liam with no choice but to make up his mind about what he would do. He only had two options: jumping off or riding the train to wherever it had planned to stop. The train was still going slow enough that he was sure he could jump off, but he sat momentarily, tightening his backpack onto his shoulder, thinking about how someone might jump off a moving train. If he could jump far enough, he would not worry about being crushed by the following train cars.

All at once, Liam remembered many years ago when his fourth-grade class had gone on a school field trip to the mill, which included a tour of the train yard. He could remember the man saying to the class, "If you ever find yourself needing to jump off a moving train, always jump onto your left foot, then you'll spin away from the car. Jump on your right foot, you'll spin into the car," an old cowboy doing the tour had told the class.

"Or maybe he said it was to jump onto my right foot?" Liam spoke aloud, wishing he had paid more attention to what the man had said. "Was it the left foot? Trailing foot? What is a trailing foot?" He had no time left to think about it, so he closed his eyes and jumped as far as he could away from the train in a burst of adrenaline.

Liam hit the ground, his knees buckling on impact, sending him rolling down the small gravel hill that led away from the railroad tracks. As he slid down the gravel, the rocks bruised his side and scraped into his hands as he tried to grasp onto solid ground and come to a stop.
Finally, Liam's feet caught firm onto the grass at the bottom

of the hill from the tracks. He stood up and brushed himself off, thankful that the train was going as slow as it was. Liam sat back down for a moment, the frost on the grass soaking into his pants. He pulled out the rocks and dried grass from his hands and clothes. He gave himself a good look over, making sure he was not bleeding from anywhere and to make sure he did not have any bones sticking out where they should not be.

Liam walked down the rest of the hill along the train tracks, trenching through the thick grass and uneven dirt until his feet were steady on the paved road. He looked around; within his eyes reach he could see the city, marked by streetlights along the straight edges of city roads and tall buildings marking the city lines. He could see the moving lights of busy cars driving along the main streets, spreading across the city like ants across an anthill. Liam strapped his backpack tightly against his shoulders and set off, walking down the main road that he could see heading straight through the center of town. He had only been to Boulder Ridge a few times before, but that had been enough to know that the high school, like in most small towns, should be easy to find on the main road.

Liam turned his face from the wind, zipping his jacket up to the bridge of his nose, and began walking. Passing the sign that he had read twenty minutes before. Liam turned to look at it and read it aloud, "Now Leaving Boulder Ridge; see you soon," Liam laughed to himself, "Yeah, see you real soon, Boulder Ridge." He chuckled to himself again. "Oh man, I must be tired."

He walked a reasonable distance before stopping, his feet starting to feel heavy and slow as his walk turned to a trudge. Although he was excited, with each step the more nervous he also became. His nerves hit his empty stomach, which loudly echoed its complaints. Liam reached into his jacket pocket, remembering that he still had the chocolate bar that Mr. Lister had given him the day before. Liam ate his snack, which seemed to settle him as he hastened his pace, continuing along the main road for quite a distance. His heart raced with anticipation as a large sign ahead came into view that read, 'Brookeside High School.'

"8:41," Liam confirmed, tapping the face of his watch.

The front entrance had four steps to the front door, and on each side were black hand railings. Leading up to the stairs were sidewalks, and between the sidewalk and the school was a flower bed filled with woodchips, cedar trees, and dried flowers that had long lost their bloom. The flower bed was outlined by bricks, and to the left was a large flag pole, with the red and white Canadian flag flying proudly in the breeze. Liam walked up the sidewalk, feeling a surge of nerves growing with each step, threatening to give away his facade. He watched the kids hustle inside the front door, looking like a regular morning at his school. As Liam continued up the walkway, he quickly stopped, realizing that on his long trip to the school, he had not spent any time thinking up a plan for how he was going to actually get inside. He knew it would be easy enough to just walk inside the school, blending in seamlessly with the others in the hallway. But what was his plan after that?

Liam stopped by the flag pole, allowing kids to pass him as they went up the stairs and into the front doors. He grabbed the camera from his pocket, but did not notice the wrapper from his earlier snack had fallen from it. He was distracted, deciding to take some pictures of the school and the buses that lined up opposite the front entrance that kids were now spilling out of. He was hoping for a plan to just dawn on him without much more thought, because the more that he tried to think of one, the emptier his mind felt.

"Hey, mister!" a sharp voice spoke sternly from behind him, tapping him on the shoulder. "Littering is bad for the earth!"

Liam twirled around, nearly jumping out of his skin, his loud heart knocking steadily on his Adam's apple. There stood a girl, about a head shorter than Liam, with strawberry blond, chin-length hair that flicked out at the ends. Her face had a smattering of freckles, and her green eyes were hooded by her scowling brow, low with disappointment. Liam looked at her arm stretched out towards him, and in her hand was a candy wrapper that Liam recognized as his own. His face flashed red, realizing it must have dropped out of his pocket when he grabbed the camera. Liam swallowed hard as he lifted his hand to hers, catching his accidentally discarded wrapper from her outreached hand.

"Oh, sorry," Liam's voice went meek, burying the wrapper deep in his jeans pocket.

"Why are you shaking?" the girl's face cracked into a smile. "Do you got something to hide?"

"No, sorry," Liam laughed as he wiped the sweat from his brow. "You just scared me!"

The girl laughed back, but hers was less of a nervous laugh than Liam's. "So, you're some random kid taking pictures of school kids at a school that he doesn't go to, and *I'm* scaring *you?*"

"What? People take pictures all the time," Liam insisted, his nerves pulling on the cords of his voice box.

"Not me. People take pictures of things they want to remember. There isn't anything worth remembering around here for me," she answered.

"Well, I disagree," Liam bantered. "Sometimes pictures are all we have left."

"Oh great, cryptic, wanna-be wise answers when all I asked for was clarity!" The girl said, throwing her hands into the air dramatically.

"Besides, what makes you think I don't go here?" Liam asked, wondering what had given him away.

"I'm on the yearbook committee," she argued. "I've seen every face that goes here."

"You're on the yearbook committee, but you never take any pictures?" Liam laughed. "Seems weird, but okay. Maybe I'm new here!"

"Nope," she continued to argue. "You aren't. Just tell me what you're doing here, and maybe I'll just pretend I didn't see you and won't tell the principal that some weirdo is hugging the flag pole and taking pictures of her students."

"Okay, calm down." Liam said, not old enough to know that telling someone to 'calm down' is never a way to get them to actually calm down. "I'm looking for someone."

"Calm down? You calm down! I'm just asking you some questions. Who are you looking for? Maybe I can help you find them," the girl persisted, not seeming convinced.

This girl had nothing threatening about her besides her attitude. She was not tall, and she did not look very strong underneath her oversized sweater and baggy jeans. Liam wondered if accepting her offer was a good idea or not, but as he heard the school bell ring, he realized that he needed to get inside the school somehow, and she was the only person to offer to help him. Her green eyes fiercely sized Liam up through her hair, which hung partly over her eyes and nose.

"It's a lot to explain. I don't actually know his name," Liam tripped over his own words, feeling how foolish Jacob must have felt when he tried to explain all of this to him. "I just know that they go here, so I need to figure out a way to get into the school."

"Looking for someone, hey?" she said, eyeing him suspiciously. "What's your name?"

"Liam," he responded, somewhat reluctantly. He was unsure if he should give her his real name or make something up.

"Well, Liam," the girl folded her arms across her chest and dropped her left hip, looking over him from head to toe. "This seems like a funny story. I like funny stories. Liam, tell us a funny story."

"Do you think you can get me into the school or not?" Liam said, trying to cover his frustration. All the kids had run into the school, and the two stood alone outside. Any chance of slipping in seamlessly with the other kids was gone, and now whatever plan she had was the only plan.

"I'll tell you what. You buy me some lunch from the cafeteria today, and I'll get you in the school with no questions asked. Well…" the girl paused momentarily, "actually maybe they'll be some questions asked."

"How are you going to do that?" Liam asked.

"Don't worry about how. Do we have a deal or what?" she asked again, as if to indicate that the offer was about to expire.

"Deal. Now, how are you going to get me in?"

"Just come with me. We'll wing it," she said, waving her hand toward the front door.

Chapter 7

~ Shared Secrets ~

Liam followed her, but was beginning to wonder if she could actually help him. She seemed very blunt, and it made Liam nervous. His mission was an important one, and he did not see how someone *'winging it'* would help him at all. He even wondered if maybe she was trying to set him up for her own entertainment, and there was something in the way she skipped past him and up to the front doors, swinging them open before looking back to Liam. She was looking annoyed as she nodded her head at the open door, signaling Liam to follow her.

"What is your name, anyway?" Liam asked, stopping with her just inside the open door.

"My name is Brynn, Brynn McFarlay! It's good to meet you!" she was now turned with both shoulders towards him, standing board straight and holding her hand to Liam. Liam was unsure if she was being sarcastic, making fun of him, or if this was just her usual way of introducing herself. Reluctantly, Liam lifted his arm out and met her grip on his own, shaking her hand. "It's nice to meet you too, Brynn McFarlay. Does everyone call you Brynn McFarlay, or can I call you Brynn?" Liam asked, still shaking her hand, matching what he'd made up his mind to be sarcastic.

"You can call me…."

Before Brynn could finish her sentence, she accidentally hit another student walking through the doorway as she pulled her hand back from Liam and back to her side.

"Watch it, Barley!" The other student yelled back at her.

"Barley?" Liam laughed. "They call you Barley?"

Brynn looked like she was going to smack Liam's face right off his head. "Yes. And I hate it, so don't you dare!" Brynn walked out of the doorway and started walking down the busy hallway.

Liam followed quickly behind her, finally catching up to her as she stopped at a locker. "How does someone get a nickname like Barley?" he asked, biting his lip to prison his laugh.

"Just the same way anyone gets a nickname," Brynn looked at what Liam would call tense, and she spoke in a harsh tone. It was clear to Liam that she was getting even more annoyed than he had intended to make her. "Why does it even matter? You can call me Brynn, and maybe someday I'll tell you how I got the nickname. But it's on a need-to-know basis, and right now, you don't need to know!" Brynn turned away from Liam, slammed her locker door, and walked down the hallway again.

"Well, if it makes you feel any better, my brothers called me chicken legs when I was a kid," Liam shared, hoping that this embarrassing story would relieve some of her irritability with him.

Brynn stopped and turned to Liam again. Her eyes narrowed, and her lip twitched. She took a moment to think before she eventually responded. "That does make me feel better, so if you call me Barley, I'm going to call you Chicken Legs. Deal?"

Liam nodded and smiled as the two walked down the hallways and headed toward their first class. Brookeside High

School was larger than Liam's. The hallways seemed wider, and even the ceiling seemed to tower above Liam's head. School pride was everywhere. The walls were lined with trophy cases and awards, and they all looked freshly painted, with the school mascot, a lion, painted everywhere. Walking on the floor, no one was tripping over shifted floors or broken tiles.

When Liam was called upon by the teachers wondering why he was there. Brynn told one that he was her cousin from out of town, staying with her family while his parents settled their divorce in court. To another, she said he was a foster kid that her parents had taken in. Whatever the reason gave, Liam could tell that Brynn was having far too much fun thinking of reasons for him to be there, always adding an embarrassing detail or two just to poke fun at him. Each teacher had the same look of frustration written all over their face, wondering why the office had not let them know a new student would be joining them, but most of them never pressed the matter further than that and just told him to take a seat at an empty desk.

The first class of the day was English, taught by Mr. Williams, an average-looking man with a slender build and curly, frizzy light brown hair that made his thick, dark eyebrows look out of place and almost glued on. He wore an argyle pattern sweater with a mix of beige and brown woven into the pattern. Matched with his brown hair and brown sweater vest were Mr. Williams' brown pants, which looked like they were made of wool, and lastly, his brown, shiny shoes.

As Liam walked behind Brynn and went to sit beside her, Mr. Williams stood up in a hurry and quickly called Liam and Brynn, both to his desk at the front of the classroom. As they approached him, Brynn explained that Liam was her cousin. Mr. Williams' eyes narrowed to slits as he looked at Liam through his thick, bushy eyebrows. It was clear that he was not happy, but Liam was not sure if he was just an unhappy man or if he was unhappy with him. Mr. Williams said nothing as he looked over Liam, making for an awkward, long moment. The furrows in Mr. Williams' forehead deepened as he tried to decide if he liked the look of him or if he looked like he would be causing trouble for his class, but he eventually told them both to take a seat.

Liam sat next to Brynn at an empty desk, and within just a few minutes from the start of class, Mr. Williams had the entire classroom taking turns
reading Shakespeare's Romeo and Juliette. Mr. Williams walked around the classroom, his hands folded behind him under the small of his back, calling on each student when it

was their turn to read a paragraph as he mouthed every word from memory. At times, students would take a moment while reading, struggling with all the 'thus,' and 'wherefore art thou's' that felt unnatural and unfamiliar to them. Mr. Williams, without pausing, would recite the following line, sometimes closing his eyes as he spoke, as if it was somewhat of an emotional nostalgia. At the end of class, Mr. Williams dismissed them, telling them to finish reading the second act for class on Monday.

Liam had done it. He had snuck into a foreign school and sat through an entire class, and a bolt of excitement ran through him. "What class is next?" Liam asked.

"Next is science," Brynn answered. "Science is my favourite."

"Science is definitely not my strongest subject," Liam said to Brynn as they rounded a corner in the hallway and entered a classroom with the heading "Science Lab—Miss Evans."

"Mine either, really," Brynn replied.

"I thought you just said science is your favourite class?"

"It is, but not because I like the work," Brynn stated. "Mr. Peterson was the science teacher here for twenty years, until last month he won the lottery and quit, and now probably sitting on his own private island. Miss Evans took over his class after he left. The school must have scrambled to find someone because she's definitely not a good teacher. I don't think she's ever taught anyone anything before.

But she's the funniest teacher ever! She always mispronounces all the scientific terms, and the entire class has bets placed on how many words a class she'll mispronounce! It sounds ruthless, but it's too funny not to! But luckily, we're still reviewing all the stuff that Mr. Peterson taught us last year, but once she starts trying to teach us new stuff, we'll probably all be hooped."

Brynn and Liam exchanged laughs as they took their seats at a large, green table on the left side of the classroom next to a window. The classroom was loud, and kids were throwing paper airplanes around and shouting over one another—completely different from the quiet and reserved English class that they had just left.

Miss Evans came into the science lab five minutes late, emptying her full arms onto her desk and dropping some papers and pens onto the floor as she did. "Hello, class," she said, out of breath, pulling her dark curls away from her face, trying to compose herself. "Today we will be continuing our worksheets on microbiology. Please open your textbooks to…." She quickly flipped through the pages of the textbook on her desk, finally landing on the correct page and reading from it, "To the… annie-rob-y?" Miss Evans struggled more with each try, "the anny-robbin heading."

The class roared with laughter, some kids making check marks on their bet papers that they had come prepared for class with. Confused, Miss Evans lifted her head from the textbook, looking around from behind a curtain of curls that had fallen again over her red face. Brynn side-eyed Liam, nudging him as they hid their smiles in the textbook. "I told you!" Brynn whispered and laughed, "She means anaerobe!"

Miss Evans stood up, her arms stretched, her hands flat on the desk, as she looked around the classroom. Her eyes caught on Brynn, who was still laughing and whispering to Liam, "Brynn?" Miss Evans yelled across the commotion, trying anything to regain control of the classroom. "Do you want to tell the class what you're whispering about?" Brynn looked over her textbook, which she had tried hiding behind, and placed it flat on the table. "Nope!" Brynn smirked at Miss Evans. "That was why I was whispering!" Brynn crossed her arms and shrugged back into her chair, looking at Liam as if feeling some accomplishment from what she had said.

The classroom erupted into laughter again. Miss Evans lifted her hands from her desk, tucking her hair behind her ear. Her entire face went red again, this time with anger. Miss Evans walked around her desk and towards Brynn, who was still smirking at her.

Just as she was about to give her an earful of trouble, she noticed Liam sitting beside Brynn and said, "Who is this with you today?"

"This is my cousin, Liam. His family is moving to town, and he's staying with me while his parents pack up their house and make the trip across the country."

"Oh," Miss Evans said with surprise, but she brushed the look off her face, trying to hide her frustration from Liam, and continued, "Well, I don't have another textbook for you to work with, so you'll have to share with Brynn."

"That's fine, thank you," Liam said as politely as he could after Brynn had been so impolite to her. He pulled his chair closer to face Brynn so that they both could see the textbook.

Miss Evans walked slowly back to her desk, realizing halfway there that she had forgotten to give Brynn the trouble she was due. But since she and Liam were now working quietly into their textbook, and the rest of their class had settled in as well, she decided to just sit back down at her desk and let them work, which is how the remainder of the class was spent.

Although everything felt new and exciting to Liam, why he was there was never far from his mind. He wondered if he had been in a classroom with Railway Diaries yet and was glad that he had made it through almost two classes without any real pushback from any of the teachers. He thought Brynn was his best bet to make it through the rest of the day, no matter how impulsive she was. He figured that if he could make it through two classes so far, the rest of the day should go smoothly. But he was wrong.

Chapter 8

~Confronted By Authority~

As the class worked quietly, a static voice came overhead, "Brynn McFarlay, Brynn McFarlay, please come to the office."

Liam looked at Brynn, the nerves crawling on his face.

The static cracked again as the voice came overhead. "And bring your cousin with you."

The room was filled with "ooooo" and "awwwws" of the other students at Brynn as they walked through the classroom and into the hallways. Brynn just rolled her eyes as she walked by them, and Liam watched his feet as he dragged them nervously down the hallway and toward the office. The two walked from the hallway and into the main office. A short, round woman was sitting behind the desk with a headset on top of her puffy red hair.

"Oh, Brynn McFarlay, thanks for coming here so quickly," the lady squeaked in an almost unnaturally high but friendly way. "Principal Meyers is just on the phone, but she'll call you right in when she's finished. Okay? Please take a seat." The lady smiled beneath her thick layers of red lipstick, holding out her hand towards the benches. "And remember, kids, she's your princi-*pal*."

"Thanks, Mrs. Oliver," Brynn nodded her head to the lady, and she and Liam took a seat on the benches next to the office desk. The phone rang, and Liam tried to listen in, thinking maybe it could be a reason why they were now sitting and waiting for the principal. Liam was almost positive that he and Brynn had been called to the office because Drew had somehow found him, and after calling the school, the teachers realized that Liam was actually not Brynn's cousin, and now they were both in big trouble. He sat quietly, not even responding to Brynn, who was chatting about something that did not seem important to Liam

then. Liam's head felt sweaty, and his heart was pounding throughout his entire body.

"Thank you for calling Brookeside High School. Mrs. Oliver is speaking. How may I help you today?" Liam overheard. Mrs. Oliver's eyes wandered as she listened to the conversation on the other end of her headset. "Okay," she said. "Yes," she answered again. Mrs. Oliver's fake long nails clicked away at the keyboard in front of her. "Okay, so Richard Terry will be picked up for a doctor's appointment at lunch today…." Liam sighed as he realized that the conversation had nothing to do with him, and then he stopped listening. But he could still hear the squeak of Mrs. Oliver's voice as she spoke on.

Brynn must have noticed Liam was upset, so she tried her best to distract him. " So," she started, "are you going to tell me who you're looking for yet? Maybe I can help other than just getting you into the school."

Liam welcomed her positivity, but he himself felt derailed by the fact that the two were now sitting outside of the office, waiting for the principal.

"I don't know their name or anything,
but I'm looking for who painted this," Liam leaned down to the floor where his backpack was sitting. Then, grabbing the camera, he began looking through Jacob's pictures until he got to the picture of the giant octopus stretched across the train car. Liam turned the camera towards Brynn.

Brynn grabbed Liam's camera to take a closer look. "Oh! I've seen a drawing that looks similar to that one," Brynn announced, handing the camera back to Liam. "It's on an art project outside Ms. Gordon's classroom."

"Really?" Liam said excitedly. "If we make it out of this, will you show me?"

"Not until you tell me why. Obviously, you don't work for the train company, so why do you care about some train art?" she asked.

"My brother was friends with this person. He called him Railway Diaries."

"Was?" Brynn asked. "What are you here to settle his debt or something?"

"Was, yes," Liam drew in a deep breath, "my brother died two days ago," he continued, his voice cracking under the weight of his words. He only now realized that had been the first time he had said out loud that his brother had died.

"I'm sorry about your brother, Liam."

Liam reached into the front pocket of his backpack, lifting out the still-sealed envelope. "He left this for them." Brynn tried to grab it, but Liam pulled back, placing the envelope back in his bag. "It's for Railway Diaries," Liam continued. "So I have to find him and give it to him."

Liam placed his backpack on the floor before sitting up and resting his head against the wall that lined the bench they were sitting on. He opened his eyes again, and as he did, something carved into the wall next to him caught his attention, and he was now more excited than he was scared. Liam ran his hand against the etching in the wall before picking up his backpack from his feet, quickly ruffling through and grabbing his camera again. He shuffled through the pictures again, zooming into one with the signature. His eyes shifted from the camera to the wall and back to the camera again. He thought maybe he was seeing things, so he blinked his eyes tightly, but his eyes were not playing tricks on him.

"What are you doing?" Brynn asked him, only now noticing his strange behavior.

"Look!" he said to her. "Whoever carved this into the wall here is the same person who signed this train art!" Liam zoomed even more into the bottom corner and showed it to Brynn: "It's the exact same signature!"

Brynn looked at the camera and again at the wall. "Are you sure that's even a signature?" she asked unenthusiastically, handing the camera back to Liam.

Liam nodded. "It's in every picture that my brother took. It's how he recognized that all the train art was by the same person."

Brynn looked again, shrugging her shoulders, "Huh, so whoever you're looking for spends a lot of time waiting for the principal. Are you still sure you want to find them?"

Brynn looked at Liam, noticing how nervous still he was, his foot tapping away as he waited for the office door to open. "Well, now we have our first two clues. That's something!" She continued, "Now we'll have our own code words. We'll call this 'Operation Railroad,' or do you prefer 'Operation Railway Diaries'? Operation RD?" Brynn thought about those names for a moment but then started shaking her head, looking at Liam to see if he could come up with something better.

"You really want to help me find this person?" Liam asked.

Brynn nodded, her look suggesting that it should have been obvious that she wanted to.

"My older brother Drew thought it was a wild goose chase," Liam said. Thinking about Drew made him even more nervous, reminding him that he was sitting outside the principal's office, and he half expected Drew to walk into the room at any moment.

"Well, I'm in this now!" Brynn answered. "I'm fully invested, wild goose chase or not."

Liam smiled at Brynn. "Thank you. I'll let you come up with the names for the operation. But let's start by showing me the art project that you were just talking about first."

Brynn patted her hand on the bench they were sitting on. "Maybe you forgot where we are? *First,* we have to wait for the principal."

The two sat a while longer until the door opened to the principal's office, and the two were summoned inside by a tall woman with wavy blonde hair that framed her narrow face and her smile that showed all her teeth at once and when she spoke, her voice was soft and kind. She asked them to sit down in the empty chairs across the desk from her.

Principal Meyer's office reminded Liam more of Mr. Wydler's office than it did his own principal's. Everything was neatly arranged, and the light from the outside window brought in a natural, warm glow. Instead of pictures of children on her desk, every frame was filled with her and a big black dog. The walls were lined with more school pride, of basketball and volleyball teams and trophies, framed newspaper clippings that celebrated her school and her own degrees in education. The far wall in front of the window was lined with black filing cabinets, and tucked into the corner was a large desk, with two computer monitors to one side with generic screen savers playing across them, and on the other side were neatly arranged files sitting in a basket.

"Hello again, Brynn," Principal Meyers said before pulling out her chair and seating herself across from them. "I've brought you and your cousin to discuss a few things with you."

All of Liam's experience with principals had been with Principal Johnson, and with those experiences, Liam thought that they all must be the same, so despite her kind voice, he wondered if she was as kind in deed as she sounded when she spoke. Liam swallowed loudly over the lump in his throat but said nothing. The awkward silence felt longer than it should, but it was only a few seconds before Brynn spoke.

"What can we do for you, Principal Meyers?"

"Well, first, let me introduce myself to your cousin," Principal Meyers said, looking at Liam, her warm smile seeming genuine and gentle. "I'm Principal Meyers. What is your name?"

"Liam, Liam Robertson," he answered quickly.

"And where are you from?"

"I'm from Larsen Creek," Liam answered truthfully, trying not to trip himself in a lie.

"Well, welcome to Brookeside High School, Liam."

Liam smiled, "thank you," he said, relaxing more now, he was almost convinced Principal Meyers was as genuine as she seemed.

"Now, Brynn," Principal Meyers turned her attention and folded hands that rested on her desk towards Brynn, who was quietly sitting next to Liam, "I've gotten a couple of complaints from your teachers this morning about your cousin coming into class unannounced today and tried to say that it was Mrs. Oliver's fault for not letting them know about your parent's call to the school office to let us know that your cousin would be joining us," Principal Meyers leaned in, still speaking with a kind smile on her face, "But Brynn, your parents never did call. No one let the school know that your cousin would be joining us today. Now, as you can imagine, this is a problem."

Principal Meyers stood up from her desk, and Liam felt a cold thrill fall down his spine. He was sure that this was where Principal Meyers would show her true intentions now, as most of those who stood in authority over him had done. Her kind façade would be replaced with her true face, and his mission would be over just as it was beginning to gain

traction.

Chapter 9

~Clue on the Canvas~

As Principal Meyers stood at the front of her desk, Liam felt himself slipping deep into the back of his chair. Principal Meyers did not stand over them but instead walked to a cabinet in the corner of her office and pulled from the top drawer a folder marked 'Brynn McFarlay' and sat back down in her chair, putting the folder on the desk. She opened the folder, thumbing her way through a few pages as Liam and Brynn sat nervously in front of her.

"We've tried calling your parents to clear up this…. Misunderstanding," Principal Meyers smiled again, opening Brynn's file to a page with her parents' contact information. "But your parents aren't answering their phones. Is there someone else, maybe your cousin's parents? Just someone to confirm that he is okay to be here."

Brynn looked at her oddly thick file on the desk and thought for a moment, rising from her chair as she spoke. "My parents are out of town, and Liam's parents are…. Liam's parents are with them!"

"Let me make sure I understand what you're saying here, Brynn. Your parents and Liam's parents left town, leaving your cousin," Principal Meyers nodded and gestured her hand towards Liam, "and you home alone. All while expecting for him to go to school until they got home, and no one thought it might be a good idea to call the school to let us know?"

"That's pretty much right," Brynn said as reassuringly as she could. "I'm sure they tried to call. Have you checked your voicemail?"

"Yes, Miss McFarlay, we've checked our voicemail, and there was nothing about Liam joining us for…." Principal Meyers turned towards Liam. "Well, that's a good point as well. How long did your parents plan on you joining us, Liam?"

"uhm," Liam paused, looking at Brynn to help him out.

"I think just today. Maybe all of next week, too! Then he should be all moved to his new town!" Brynn said.

"Where are you and your family moving to, Liam?" Principal Meyers asked.

"…uhm," he paused, "they, they didn't say."

Brynn closed her eyes, shaking her head in disbelief at what Liam had just said. Liam could see her trying to find the words to recover the conversation so Principal Meyers would not be shocked by Liam's nonsense.

"Your parents didn't tell you where you're moving to?" Principal Meyers asked, her brow flat with skepticism, her eyes fixed on Liam.

"Who doesn't like a surprise!?" Brynn laughed, trying to distract Principal Meyers from Liam, whose face was nearly sweating bullets now.

"Right," Principal Meyers said. "Well, since we can't exactly kick you loose onto the streets, you can spend the day in class with Brynn. But without confirmation from either Brynn's parents or from your own, that's all we can do for you. If you expect to come next week, I will need, at the very least, a phone call from your parents. As long as the two of you don't get into any trouble. Do you two understand me? If you two get into trouble, I'll have you do your schoolwork on my office floor. Do I make myself clear?"

The two nodded aggressively, ensuring they showed her that they understood and that there was no room for misunderstanding. Principal Meyers thanked them for coming in and opened her office door, excusing them both. They walked past Mrs. Oliver, who was busy clunking away at her computer and laughing on her headset.

Brynn smacked Liam on the arm as soon as the two were out of the office's view. *'They didn't tell me where we're moving,'* she mocked. "What the heck, man!"

"I'm sorry," Liam said, rubbing his sore arm. "I panicked!"

"It's almost lunch," Brynn announced when they reached the hallway. "Let's walk down to the art class, and I'll show you that octopus painting I was telling you about."

Liam looked along the walls as he walked down the hallway. These walls were adorned with trophies and medals, class pictures, and class projects. Liam still felt surprised not to see any flickering lights as they walked down the hall, or weird smells coming from the cafeteria, and how everything looked fresh, probably in any light. Brynn stopped outside an empty classroom door, pointing to where the art projects were displayed on the wall.

"These are all the art class projects so far this year," she said.

Liam scanned the paintings. One was an orange and black butterfly riding on a green kite against a blue sky. Another was a pink bulldog wearing sunglasses, and then, staring back at him, a purple octopus stretched across the white paper.

Liam felt a rush of excitement and nearly pulled the drawing off the wall. "Who drew this?"

It was not exactly like the picture on Jacob's camera, but it was close enough that Liam felt fairly certain that they could have been done by the same artist.

Brynn lifted the paper to read the writing on the back: "It says here it was drawn by Mark Peters."

"Mark Peters. Do you know him? Do you know where he is? Is he in any of your classes?" Liam asked in rapid succession.

"He was here earlier! He was in homeroom, but I didn't see him in English, so I'm guessing he skipped. The kids say…Oh my gosh!" Brynn exclaimed loudly.

"What?" Liam said with a startle.

"I've heard some of the kids say that he likes to hang out by the train tracks and that he likes tagging train cars down there."

"Why didn't you tell me that when I showed you the pictures of all the train car art?"

"I didn't think about it. You were so excited about that signature, but that signature doesn't look like anything I could see Mark using."

"The signature!" Liam interrupted, looking back at the painting on the wall. Scanning over the picture for any trace of a signature. "This picture doesn't have any signature."

"Well, we could probably wait for Mark to come back. I mean, there's nothing to say he's gone to the train yard for sure anyway," Brynn said.

"I'd really like to check out the train yard. There might be even more clues there, too," Liam replied.

"Well, maybe we should skip next period and go to the train yard instead. Even if Mark isn't there now, chances are that he won't be back in class to ask until the end of the day, anyway. That's what all the kids do when they skip. They always make sure they're back for the last class. We can corner him back here at the end of the day."

"I don't know," Liam
shrugged. "I don't think I've ever skipped class before. Well, I guess I left school yesterday," he realized. "But that seems different because they told me not to come in for a few days, so that doesn't even count as skipping," he reasoned.

"Oh, come on, Liam," Brynn
groaned, "you don't actually go to this school,

so you're technically not even skipping classes. Jeesh!" She exclaimed, "Do you seriously always play everything so safe?"

Liam rolled his eyes and groaned, "I'm so tired of everyone telling me I play everything so safe. I jumped on a train in the middle of the night to come to another town and to another school that I've never been to! Does any of this sound like something someone would do that always plays everything safe?"

Brynn smiled, "Okay there, Mr. Dangerous. So, we skip the next class to go to the train yard."

Liam agreed with a nod.

"But let's stay for lunch. You said you'd buy me some food from the cafeteria," Brynn reminded. "And I'm starving."

While the two walked down the halls, the lunch bell rang, and the hallways were busting with students again. The cafeteria opened from the hallway into a large room twice the size of the gymnasium at Liam's school. Painted on the back wall was the giant lion mascot, with the black and red team colours in circles behind it. There were large windows on the far side from them looking over the outdoor basketball courtyard, and the next wall was lined with vending machines, some with drinks and others with snacks. Liam and Brynn stood in the long lunch line, which felt overly crowded, with kids shoved into each other and some even stepping on Liam's feet. Thankfully, the line moved quickly, and once they reached the end, Liam pulled out his cash and paid for both slices of pizza and chocolate milk for each of them.

"Where do you normally sit?" Liam asked, holding his food tray as he scanned the room for an empty table.

"Not at the school!" Brynn laughed. Liam looked at her, trying to see if he could discern if this was sarcasm or if Brynn was being serious.

The two spotted an empty table in the far corner of the room and went to sit down. Unlike his school lunches, the pizza was hot and not dried out at all. Even the chocolate milk had yet to expire. Liam watched Brynn as she swallowed her pizza, hardly taking the time to chew.

"Have you never eaten in your life?" Liam asked with a laugh.

Brynn seemed slightly offended but mostly embarrassed by his laugh and only shot him half a smirk in reply. Brynn finished her pizza before Liam had taken a few bites of his own. She asked him questions about his school in between his bites, making Liam take longer than usual to finish his lunch.

"So, tell me about your brother," Brynn insisted. "What was his name?"

Liam unintentionally tensed his body, feeling his toes curl in his shoes. His feelings mixed like paint. On the one hand, he felt like he did not want to talk about him, but on the other, he could go on talking about him for hours. "His name is…was," Liam stuttered, "Jacob." Liam paused momentarily while thinking about what to say about him. "He could be moody and funny, and we used to have lots of fun. Before my mom died, my oldest brother Drew used to tease him about being a 'momma's boy.' Mom used to call us all her 'sonshines,' but she did seem to show extra attention to Jacob. I didn't mind, though. I think it was because he had a hard time making friends, even in elementary school. After she died, even Drew didn't think that calling Jacob a momma's boy was funny anymore," Liam paused for a moment, nervously picking at the skin around his nails, "Jacob never really dealt with my mom's death, and it always seemed like my dad picked on him a lot more than the rest of us. He always pointed out his faults and what he thought was wrong with him. I know Jacob felt like he could do nothing right by anyone. But he really was my hero, and although he never really said it, I know he loved me." Liam pretended to brush his hair away from his face but was catching a tear that had formed in the corner of his eye before it fell down his cheek.

Liam looked up from his fidgeting fingers and at Brynn, who looked the most interested she'd ever been in anything Liam had said before. Liam had seen the look on her face before, like someone who wanted to say something but did not know what to say or how to say it. The two were quiet for a moment.

"If you don't mind me asking," Brynn began after a long pause, "why do you need to get this letter to this guy, anyway? I don't know how to ask this, but with your brother gone, isn't it a bit late for the letter, anyway?"

Liam swallowed the piece of pizza he had been chewing and answered, "I just know that my brother would have wanted me to. He's gone, and I just feel like I need to finish this for him." Liam took a long sip of his chocolate milk.

"So, this is kinda your way of finding closure for what happened to him? Like a way for you to find peace with what happened to him?"

Liam put down his slice of pizza, partly because he was not very hungry after the change in topic and partly because he realized that there was no way he would have time to finish it with all of Brynn's questions, "No," he said, almost sounding offended at the idea. "This has nothing to do with me. This is just me trying to do right for my brother, to finish what he started. I don't expect to get anything from this except in a lot of trouble at home."

"It's not about the destination, Liam; it's all about what you learn on the journey," Brynn said, sounding like she was quoting something she had once heard.

"This isn't some fantasy novel, Brynn. It's real life," Liam replied.

"Hey now," Brynn inserted, "don't be knocking fantasy novels!"

Chapter 10

~Exploring the Forgotten Tracks~

The school bell rang, announcing the end of lunch and summoning the kids back to their classes as it echoed through the hallways. Liam followed Brynn out of the lunchroom and down the hallway, trying to keep his feet from sounding as heavy as they felt. Liam felt his nerves tinge as he looked over his shoulder. He remembered clearly what Principal Meyers had threatened about them not causing trouble. He needed to make sure no one could see them as the two snuck out a side door and outside.

They walked behind the school, avoiding the large classroom windows and any main doors. It was clear to Liam that Brynn had skipped a class or two before, turning to walk along a hidden foot trail behind the shop class building and storage sheds that Liam thought could only be found if someone knew where it was. Beyond the outbuildings was a large open field, lined with what looked like fresh paint for home football games and was surrounded by bleachers. The lion mascot, with the team's red and black colours, was painted on every surface it could fit, and above them was an overhead scoreboard.

They walked until the school was far from sight, turning down from the main road onto residential streets. The train yard they were heading towards was an old pulp mill built at the same time as the Larsen Creek Mill. In its prime, it was known as the Boulder Ridge Pulp Mill, and trains would bring woodchips and other resources from one mill to the other. However, it had now been decommissioned for over ten years when the price of lumber had dipped too low. The mill was now only known as the 'train yard,' as many train cars were stored until others were dropped off and traded with others for use. It was where many kids liked to hang out, taking advantage of its secluded area for partying and underage drinking. Being one of the few places where trains would come from Larsen Creek to Boulder Ridge,

Liam felt quite sure that this would be where Jacob's letters would be picked up by Railway Diaries.

Walking down these town roads felt no different to Liam than his own streets back home. Like Larsen Creek, Boulder Ridge was not a very large town, and it did not take long before Brynn announced that they were almost there. It was primarily residential roads, with a town center that held most of the stores and a small mall, and for entertainment was a small, one-screen movie theatre. On the outskirts were most of the industrial buildings and businesses and a small airport that, on average, only saw one plane leave a day.

As they walked, they made small talk about school and the differences and similarities between the towns. Brynn was excited to learn all about Liam's school and laughed at the idea of having such a ridiculous principal. After some time, Liam noticed that Brynn had gotten quiet. He'd tried to engage her in more conversation, but she only offered one-word answers, if any at all. All of what Liam knew from Brynn so far told him that this was not normal for her. He had spent most of the time trying to keep up with her in conversation, and now he could barely get her to mutter a word.

"What's up?" Liam finally asked.

"What?" Brynn asked, as if not realizing that her behavior had shifted.

"What made you suddenly go so quiet?" Liam asked and then laughed. "You being this quiet makes me nervous."

Brynn was quiet for a while longer, and she kept looking at Liam like she was trying to think of what to say until finally she did. "I gotta tell you something, Liam," Brynn announced.

"Yeah? What's that?" Liam asked.

"I should have told you this before," Brynn's voice dropped. "But you might not have wanted to go if I had."

Brynn stopped walking and waited for Liam to say something. Liam stopped a few steps ahead of her and turned back to look at her, his face strained with concern.

"What are you talking about?" Liam asked again. "Now you're really starting to make me nervous!"

"Okay, I'll just tell you. But you can't be mad that I didn't tell you before we left. Okay, so, the train yard we're walking to... it's…" Brynn stumbled over her words, fidgeting with her sweaty palms.

"It's what?"

"Well, it's haunted!" Brynn spat out.

"Haunted?" Liam laughed. He was relieved at the ridiculousness of the statement and slowly started walking again. "Like what, ghosts?"

Brynn nodded her head quickly, with a look on her face that said the answer should have been obvious.

Liam laughed again, trying to figure out if Brynn was joking. The look on her face said that she was not. "Ghosts?" he asked again. "You're serious?"

"Yes, haunted with ghosts," Brynn had stopped on the sidewalk. "What, you don't believe in ghosts?"

Liam continued walking, but turned to Brynn, who was still stalled. "I have a theory that only people who believe in ghosts have ever seen a ghost. So, no, I've never seen a ghost, and I don't believe in them, either."

"Well, I've never seen a ghost either!" Brynn ran to catch up to Liam, "but that's why most kids sneak down to the train yard, to catch a glimpse of it. It's like an urban legend around here. They say the ghost that haunts the yard was a homeless man who was hit by a car, but others say that he was the train conductor there in the eighties, that jumped from a moving, burning train, and now haunts the yard."

"I'm guessing that most kids go to the train yard to skip school and party. Besides," Liam added, "I jumped from a moving train, and I'm not a ghost. There seems to be a flaw in the logic of your ghost story," Liam laughed again.

"All I'm saying is that a bunch of kids have seen ghosts, and I thought you'd want to know. A few years ago a kid here went missing, and everyone thinks that he was taken by the ghosts."

"Really?" Liam asked, startled. "A kid went missing from the train yard?"

"No one really knew where he went missing from. He was found later in the day in his basement, playing video games. His mom had to make a public apology on the news for causing such a scene over her missing son and everything. But some still think he was taken by the ghosts." Brynn looked at Liam, to whom her story had clearly lost all credibility, and said, "Well, I'm so sorry for trying to be a good friend and not wanting you to go missing, too."

"Well, thank you for letting me know," Liam said with all the sincerity he could muster. "I appreciate having such a good friend."

"Boulder Ridge Pulp Mill LTD," read a large sign that stood at the side of a long, winding gravel road lined with trees. The white paint was now peeling off the wooden sign, and the gravel road was choked with weeds, evident that it had not been used in quite some time, or at least not often. As the two entered the yard, Liam could see that the walls of the decaying buildings were full of graffiti, and the windows were mostly all broken. Liam and Brynn walked beside the main building, where there was a large, makeshift firepit constructed from piles of old pallets and wood ripped off the outside of the buildings. With no maintenance, overgrown plants had taken over most of the yard, and rows and rows of train cars lined the tracks. If Liam allowed himself, he could probably understand why the kids all claimed it was haunted and kept to himself that the empty lot could conjure fear into anyone. Liam inhaled a deep breath, swallowing his nerves. He walked on, with Brynn standing oddly close beside him.

Liam and Brynn watched their feet as they walked towards the tracks. The ground was covered with nails, garbage, and various chunks of metal and wood. As they walked along the side of a long line of train cars, they looked over all the graffiti and art that canvased over the sides of them. Some were abstract shapes, others were large, intricate murals of bright colours and rebellious expressions, and others were hastily scrawled tags hidden in the shadows of corners or between the cars. They walked together through rows and rows, Liam taking pictures of any that he found to be interesting or that may be important. Then, Liam and Brynn were startled to see someone just ahead of them, dressed all in black with their hood pulled over their face and a spray can rattling in their hand as they shook it.

Together, the two bolted between two train cars where they would be out of sight. "There's someone over there!" Liam whispered, his back slamming against the train car.

"Wow, you have a keen mind!" Brynn said sarcastically. "Wait!" Her voice was overcome by panic, and face flashed with fear. "Do you think it's a ghost?"

Liam flashed her a dismissing look as they leaned to have another look, ensuring they stayed hidden enough not to be seen, catching another glimpse before ducking behind again.

"That's Mark!" Brynn hissed under her breath.

"How do you know that's him?"

"Duh! I told you I know everyone, yearbook committee, remember?"

"You didn't even see his face!"

The boy that Brynn was sure was Mark was busy spray painting a train car just a few paces ahead of them. He was a wiry looking fellow, with a baseball cap on and out the sides of his hood Liam could see puffs of red hair.

"Okay, watch," Brynn peaked around again to get a better look at the person, "Hey, Mark!" she dashed back before he could entirely turn his head. "That's him for sure," she whispered back to Liam. "Looks like he's paint…" Before Brynn had even finished what she was saying, Liam passed her and was now walking out from between the train cars and was quickly heading towards Mark. Feeling a surge of adrenaline and not wanting to miss his chance, he reached into his backpack to grab the envelope as he walked.

Before Liam reached Mark, he heard the distinct sound of car tires across the gravel road from behind him. Liam turned around and saw the vehicle. It was a police car, and as soon as it was in view, Liam heard the officer turn on his sirens and drive quickly in their direction. Liam looked back to Mark, who seemed to be panicking, packing all his spray paints into his bag before jumping onto his bike and peddling off. Leaving just a trail of dust behind his tires, he passed Brynn and Liam, veering right down a side road, and was gone. Just as Mark was out of sight, the police cruiser pulled around the corner and was now right in front of Brynn and Liam, with its lights still on and siren blaring.

Chapter 11

~Caught in the Watchful Eye ~
of Officer Douglas

"We have to stay calm," Brynn whispered to Liam. "And I don't think we should tell the police about how we saw Mark out here. If we want to get anything out of him about writing these letters to your brother, we have to keep that to ourselves so we don't get Mark mad at us."

The officer was now out of his cruiser and approaching them, his lights still flashing, but he had turned off the siren. Liam looked at Brynn and in slow and steady motions, he walked closer until he was standing beside her, trying not to make any sudden movements.

Brynn looked at him. "Liam? Are you okay?" Liam's knees were nearly shaking, and he was fidgeting with his hands and, of course, looking especially suspicious.

The officer stopped less than a train car length away from them and spoke into the radio on his shoulder, "They're just a couple of kids. I may have some runners here; stand by." He walked towards the two, again stopping a few feet from them, and pulling a notepad from his front pocket. "Brynn McFarlay," the officer sucked his teeth, "I should have known that was you. What have I told you about coming up here?"

"This isn't what it looks like, Officer Douglas!" Brynn assured him.

Officer Douglas let out a single laugh. "Ha! If you knew how much I hear that in a day."

Liam nudged Brynn with his elbow, whispering under his breath, "You never told me you know this officer, and what does he mean that he's already told you not to be coming here?"

Brynn returned a nudge back into Liam's side, harder than the one he had given her. "I told you, all the kids come up here. It's not a big deal. And so, what? We've had a few run-ins before. It's not a big deal. Just relax and be quiet. Let me do the talking."

Although Liam did not have extensive experience with law enforcement, the man walking towards them looked like every police officer Liam had ever seen on TV. He wore the stereotypical aviators that covered his eyes and a thick, brown mustache that covered his top lip.

The officer took a few more steps and stood in front of them, speaking in a stern and commanding voice: "We've gotten some calls recently about kids coming up here to party, and of course, they've been spray painting the train cars. You kids know that vandalism is a big deal, don't you?"

Brynn took a big step forward towards the officer, her hands swaying from behind her to in front of her as she paced. "Yes, Officer Douglas, we were just about to call you about that," Brynn answered, trying to sound more relaxed than she was. "There *was* a kid here spray painting the train cars when we got here, but your sirens scared him off—next time, you should come in a little quieter.”

“Don’t get smart with me. I don’t see any other kids around,” Officer Douglas gestured around the train yard with the pen in his hand before fixing his eyes back on them and pointing his pen at them, “I just see you two.”

“Well, it wasn’t us, as you can see. Does it look like we have any spray paint on us?” Liam was surprised at just how calm Brynn had remained. It was either out of bravery or the practiced art of getting out of trouble, but Liam was thankful that he had Brynn there to do all the talking.

Officer Douglas shrugged and jotted some notes down on his notepad. All were silent for a few minutes. “Well, Miss McFarlay, I’ll tell you what. Consider this another warning, but when I do catch you doing whatever you’re doing up here, or the two of you are caught making any trouble at all, there isn’t going to be any amount of talking that’ll get you out of the trouble you’re going to be in, you understand me?”

“Yes, of course! But for now, we’re going to get going!” Brynn insisted, turning her back to Officer Douglas and walking back to where Liam was standing.

A look that fell over Officer Douglas's face told Liam that he found Brynn's comment disrespectful, and he did not seem like someone who took kindly to any level of disrespect, especially when it came from such a young girl. He had seen it all in his twenty years on the police force, which made minor mischief matters more annoying for him than anything. These annoying matters are probably why Brynn later told Liam that she felt he was always out to get her whenever they interacted. She explained that she always had an explanation for whatever she had found herself in when he came around, but he always said she was making up more excuses instead of hearing her reasons. The officer pulled his sunglasses off his face and tucked them into the collar of his button-up shirt and was now glaring at Brynn, and then a small grin set on his face as if he had thought of how he could punish her for her disrespect, "I'll give you kids a ride back to school. Skipping school can get you kids in a lot of trouble."

Brynn went to argue, but Liam had already started walking towards Officer Douglas' cruiser before she could say anything more to worsen their situation. As Officer Douglas opened the door to the back seat of his car, Liam's trembling hands and jello legs barely held him up. He hopped across the seat to let Brynn in behind him. He wondered if anyone else in the vehicle could hear how loudly his heart was beating or the sound of his palms squeaking together as he fidgeted. He felt like a criminal, and when he looked at Brynn, her jawline tight as she stared intensely out of the car window. Confinement of any kind seemed to insult her carefree spirit. Thankfully, it was a short drive back to the school. Liam did not think he could feel worse until they pulled up to the school, and outside the front door was a handful of students laughing at them as Officer Douglas parked and came out and around to open the door to let Brynn and Liam out.

Liam and Brynn walked as quickly as they could up the steps and to the front door, past the group of laughing kids, trying to hide their faces from the embarrassment as best they could.

"What class do you have now?" Liam asked Brynn as they reached the top step at the front door and walked inside.

"The last class on a Friday is…" Brynn thought and then snapped her finger, "Year Book! Thank goodness! Mr. Kelly hardly even stays in the class, so we won't have much work to do. Mark is in my yearbook class. Let's see if he's brave enough to show up. I'm sure that he saw us at the train yard."

Yearbook class had already begun as they walked into the computer room. Liam and Brynn exchanged smiles when they noticed Mark sitting at a computer across the room. However, he looked more surprised than excited to see them, turning his back from them as quickly as he could, clearly hoping that they did not notice him sitting there. As Liam and Brynn went to take a seat at the empty computer closest to the doorway, they could see Mark side-eyeing them as he sat with a group of his friends across the room.

"Okay, so how are we doing this?" Brynn whispered to Liam. "Good cop, bad cop?"

"Do what?" Liam asked.

"Okay, I call bad cop!" Brynn slapped her hands together, and walked towards Mark with an excited skip in her step. Once she reached Mark's desk, she put her hand down in a slam beside his keyboard.

Mark stood up in a panic, "what do you want, Barley?"

"Well, Mark. We had a pretty good talk with Officer Friendly down at the train yard this afternoon!" Brynn answered.

Mark held his finger to his lip, asking Brynn to keep her voice down as he walked away from his group of friends to speak with them. "Did you tell him it was me?"

"No," Brynn answered. "Not yet, anyway."

"Well, what? Did you take the blame?"

"Nope!"

"Okay, look, I'm sorry I just left you guys there to take the blame, but if my dad found out I was out there tagging train cars, he would take me off the football team. I've only ever been there a few times to get ideas for my own art, and I've never even done this before," Mark looked like he was being honest and had a bit of what sounded to Liam like embarrassment in his tone, "I just wanted to try it this once, I swear."

"Like we believe you've never done this before," said Brynn, in her most *bad cop,* voice, "I never understood that, you know. Why is it that all the rich kids with nice houses always want to pretend they're some sort of bad boys?"

"Wait, did you say that you've never done it before?" Liam asked.

"No, never, honest! Now look, I've answered all of your questions. Now, please don't turn me in."

"So, you're not Railway Diaries?" Liam asked.

Mark's face washed over with confusion. "Dude, I don't even know what you're talking about."

 Liam reached into his backpack and took out Jacob's camera. "This looks almost exactly the same as a picture you drew that is hanging outside the art class," Liam said, bringing the camera up to Mark's face.

Mark looked and then pushed the camera away from him. "Like I told you," Mark said, now sounding defensive. "I go to the train yard to get ideas for my own art. I've seen this car in the yard, and that's why it looks a lot like my drawing. But I did not do this one. Besides, why do you guys even care? It's not like you guys even got into trouble."

"So, it's just a coincidence that we found you out there today, the one time you decided to go down the train yard and tag?" Brynn laughed sarcastically. "Well,

I don't believe in coincidences. Now, just tell us before I beat it out of you." Brynn wiped some spit off her lip with her thumb.

Liam's mouth hung open in shock. "Okay, that's enough, Brynn," he said once he had gathered himself, pulling Brynn back a few steps.

"No, Liam, so maybe he won't bend yet," Brynn said, turning back to Mark. "But you know what they say about things that don't bend, don't you, Liam?" Brynn replied, her eyes now narrowed. Liam imagined this was for dramatic effect.

"I seriously don't know what you want me to tell you," Mark took a few steps back, trying to build some more distance between them.

"As if you really expect us to believe that? You know exactly what you have left that you can tell us. Now, how many…"

"Brynn, stop," Liam interrupted. "He's telling the truth; he's not who we were looking for." Liam turned back to Mark, both sharing the same astonished look on their faces. Thanks anyway, Mark. Sorry about all this."

Mark nodded with a half smirk, "Thanks for not ratting me out. I appreciate it."

Brynn tried to hold her ground, but Liam guided her back to their desk by both shoulders.

"You took that way too far," Liam said to Brynn once they were seated.

"What do you mean? I told you I was going to be bad cop. It was the only way to get answers from him."

"You went from a wanna-be bad cop to a wanna-be gangster real quick."

"Oh, Liam, there you go, playing it safe again."

Liam drew in a deep breath, trying not to lose his cool. "Besides, he didn't have any answers to give us. Now, if you really want to help me more, you have to let me know before you go rogue like that again."

"Well, now what?" Brynn sat back heavily, letting her head hang off the back of the chair. "That was seriously our only lead!"

"Lead?" Liam chuckled.

"Yes, lead. Haven't you ever seen a detective movie? Obviously not, or you'd know how good cop, bad cop works!" Brynn paused. "Now, we need to take a moment to think over a new plan." Brynn's squinted eyes flashed back and forth in thought. "You know who we could go and talk to? My friend Gabe! He knows this town better than anyone. He's been down every alleyway, and I'm sure he's seen every tag there is to see in this town, train car or not. He could tell us if this signature is anywhere else in town. Do you still have that half of your pizza slice?"

Liam shook his head. "No, I didn't have a container for it, so I threw it out when we left the cafeteria."

"Dang, he is usually a lot chattier after he's eaten. Probably could get more out of him with food," Brynn sat back and thought. "We will just have to stop at a pawn shop on the way down so I can get some quick cash and we'll grab a bite to eat and see if he can tell us anything. I will tell you, though, that Gabe is a little different." Brynn smiled. "Just try to keep an open mind."

Everything Brynn had said was too much for Liam to unpack, but her smile told him that she was probably up to no good and that he should brace himself for whatever was

to come.

Chapter 12

~Pawned Possessions~

The last class ended, and the school bells rang one last time. The hallways flooded once more with kids, all excited to be leaving the school for the weekend.

"Do your parents pick you up from school, or do you walk?" Liam asked Brynn as they walked out the front door.

"Dude, my mom doesn't even know what day it is, let alone where I'm at most of the time, and not that she'd care if she did. She's too busy trying to start some business selling skin care products from some company with her friend. Anyway, we're walking."

"I have to ask because I've been wondering since you said it. What did you mean when you said we'd have to stop by a pawnshop for money?" Liam asked.

"That's how I get money when I'm in a pinch," Brynn replied.

Liam's brows fell in confusion. "How do you do that?" he asked.

Brynn reached into her pocket, pulled out a green, rusted old ring, and held it in the palm of her hand to show Liam, "With this!"

"What do you mean? Someone would actually give you money to pawn that thing?"

Brynn laughed and tucked it back safely in her pocket. "We'll see," she answered.

The two walked off school grounds and down many of the same roads they had earlier in the day. They walked past the residential area and were now walking by stores and businesses in the middle of town until they stopped outside an older-looking, red brick building that had a white sign above the door that read, "Patty's Pawn Shop & Hidden Treasures." Liam followed Brynn as she stepped inside the door. The smell of old books and used clothes tickled Liam's nose, and the musk stuck to him like damp, thick air. Liam looked around, but his eyes had not yet adjusted to the bare lighting, and his senses were overloaded by everything around him. The store was packed. Not packed in the way a convenience store that was fully stocked might be, but in the way a hoarder's house might be filled, from wall to wall, with various things, clashing colours and items all piled in one place. He followed Brynn to the back of the store, where hunched over a desk sat an elderly lady with heavy-lidded eyes hidden beneath thick vintage glasses that came to sharp points at the top and a chain hanging from them and rounded the back of her neck. She clearly did not hear them come in, as noted by the startle in her voice and the small jump she made in her chair when they stood before her.

"Oh, hello," the old woman said, pulling a stray hair back into her bun, recovering herself from her startle. In a meek voice, she spoke again, "let me know if I can help you find anything." The woman then returned to the coin she was examining in her thick and knotted fingers, holding it close under her nose. As Liam and Brynn stepped closer and stood in front of the desk, the elderly woman again looked up at them, her thin lips in a natural frown as she took off her glasses and brought up a second pair that had been lying on a second beaded chain around her neck. Now that Liam and Brynn were in focus, she smiled warmly at them.

"Excuse me?" Brynn said, throwing her hands from her pockets and onto the desk. "Are you Patty? Can you help me?"

"I am, and I certainly hope that I can," said the meek voice as she put away what she was working on, taking longer than it would typically take someone to fold the coin back into the cloth. "Sorry, my arthritis is flaring up," she explained, and after placing the fabric under the desk, she lifted the hem of her dress and limped slowly around, her back hunched, her weight carried on her cane. "Did you know that there are more than one hundred different kinds of arthritis?" Patty asked once she had gotten to the other side of the desk.

"I did not," Liam answered.

Patty's face perked up with another kind smile as she looked at him. "What is it that you kids are looking for? I have ever so many things to see here. You're almost certain to find what you're looking for. We have electronics and watches. Oh, and over here, we have musical instruments," she said, building on her own enthusiasm the more she spoke, now pointing to a grey wall lined with guitars of all sizes that were featured from largest to smallest. "If it's jewelry you're looking for, I have an entire section designated just to necklaces. There are even some real pearl necklaces in on the shelf over there. Speaking of pearls, did you know that pearls were often referred to as the tears of the oyster many years ago? Oh, and speaking of pearls and oysters, did you also know that pearls are considered a very bad choice for a wedding ring because they themselves resemble tears?" She continued, more excitement in her voice the more she went on. "Oh! Speaking of wedding rings, did you know that men only started wearing wedding rings after World War II?" she spoke faster, hardly taking a moment to breathe between her sentences, her meek voice gaining momentum with every word she spoke, "Oh! But I think I know exactly what you'd like. I have this!" she shrieked, pulling two pendants from her pocket.

"Is that a four-leaf clover?" Liam asked.

"Almost!" Patty answered excitedly. "This is a three-leaf clover pendant. Four-leaf clovers are sought after as their thought to bring good luck, but three-leaf clovers," she held the pendants close to Liam and Brynn, "are reminders of hope, see, each leaf has its own meaning: faith, love, and hope. Want me to ring this up at the register for you? You look like you need some faith, love and hope," the elderly lady smiled again, and placed the pendants down on the counter.

Liam noticed the look on Brynn's face was saying that this old woman was plucking the strings of her tolerance, and he realized that she seemed to have used up her quota of patience for the day. She rolled her eyes and pulled the worn, greenly silver ring from her pocket, presenting it to Patty, interrupting her before she thought of anything else to tell them. "I'm here to sell you this," she said, placing it on the desk beside her.

Patty took the ring close to her eyes, holding it up to the dim lights, switching back to her horn-rimmed glasses for a closer look. Patty placed the ring back on the table and said regrettably, "Oh, my sweet girl, I don't think this is something I would take in my shop. I'm sorry. I do have some vintage books that I think you'll truly enjoy. They're just over here," Patty pointed to another wall in the shop, "speaking of books, did you know that the longest sentence ever written was eight hundred and twenty-three words long?"

Brynn picked the ring up, gesturing it to Patty to take it back from her. "Can you just check into it? You must have some sort of magical appraisal book or something. It's worth more than it looks," Brynn insisted.

Patty walked behind the desk again, muttering to herself about some facts about most insurance companies and how they appraise rings as she turned her back to Brynn and Liam, shuffling through some old books. While Miss Patty was distracted and Liam was not looking, Brynn reached over the front counter and into the cash drawer that sat open on the counter, filling her hands with as much cash as she could grab before stuffing it all deep into her pockets.

Slowly, Patty turned back around. "I'm sorry, dear. There's nothing in my book about this ring. I cannot take it."

"That's okay, thanks anyway." Brynn backed up towards the front door, leaving the ring, and dashed at a quick pace straight towards the door before Patty could notice the cash missing. As Brynn caught up to Liam, a golden necklace on the shelf beside her caught her eye. Brynn grabbed the necklace and stuffed it into her pocket with the cash. Brynn could hear Patty's cane tapping the floor and the slow shuffle of feet behind her as Patty yelled behind them to stop.

"Run!" Brynn yelled, pushing Liam out the door, "She can't catch us, just run!" Liam ran but was unsure why they were running until they were a block away, and then they both stopped to catch their breath.

"Why are we running?!" Liam huffed.

"Take a look!" Brynn pulled the long gold necklace and cash from her front pocket, a smile of success stuck on her face.

Liam froze, dumbfounded. His eyes were wide, and his jaw nearly hit the ground. He struggled to find any words to say to her. "You can't do that, Brynn. She…she was such a nice lady." Liam felt a pit of guilt in his stomach. "Come on, you're taking that back right now!"

"Are you kidding me? No way! She's probably already called the cops. You want Officer Douglas to show up and arrest us for real?"

"Me?! I'm not the one stealing from old ladies!" Liam exclaimed. "Now let's go! I'm not going down for being an accessory to your crime!"

"Seriously, if we take it back now, the cops will be there and will throw us in jail."

"Fine, well, give it here! I'll keep a hold on it, and we'll bring it back tomorrow. It's never too late to do the right thing," Liam said, quoting some wisdom he'd been given once that he felt compelled to share anytime it seemed fit.

Reluctantly, Brynn handed Liam the stolen items, which he then stored in his jacket pocket, closed the zipper, and checked a few times to ensure it was zipped all the way closed.

"I seriously can't believe you just did that, Brynn. Now, let's go see your friend before you break any more laws. And I'm paying for dinner!"

Together, the two walked up the sidewalk, cutting through a back alley.

Liam strolled at least three or four steps behind Brynn, but said nothing.

"Dude, why are you so mad?"

"I'm not mad. I just think…I just think that you walk too fast," Liam answered.

"You think that I walk too fast?"

"Yes, I think you walk too fast…. Fast and carelessly. So carelessly that it makes it hard to walk with you, and I think that all your fast walking is going to catch up with you someday."

"Well," Brynn paused momentarily before responding, "maybe I think you just walk too slowly! So slow that you can't get anywhere and can't keep walking this slow your entire life! I'll seriously even bet you that you've been told your whole life that you walk too slow!"

"Well, I'd rather walk slow and safely than so fast that I trample everyone around me! You walk so fast that you obviously don't care about the people walking with you! How am I supposed to walk with you?"

The two stared at each other until Brynn broke the silence. "Well, I'll make you a deal. I'll walk slower so you don't have to try to keep up anymore."

"Deal." Liam agreed, but was not sure if Brynn was even understanding him.

They set off again, at the same pace, down another side road and quickly found themselves headed up the main street again. The sidewalk on this road was busier, with people walking in and out of the stores in a hurry, advertisements in every window, and traffic going up and down the busy road. The two went around another corner and stopped in front of an electrical supply shop. Liam stretched out his arm to open the front door, and Brynn grabbed his arm. "Where are you going?"

"Aren't we going in here?

"No, we're not. Why would we be going into an electrical supply shop?"

"I don't know. When you walked up to this building, I just assumed that your friend was an electrician or something. Or maybe he was a city worker or something, and that's why he knows the town so well."

"Well, you know what they say about when you assume?" Brynn laughed at her own joke. "Gabe isn't an electrician, and he doesn't work for the city either." Brynn walked past the door to the side of the building. "He's usually around back here this time of day," Brynn said.

The two walked along the front of an older-looking building, its paint weathered and wood nearly splintering from neglect. Although most of the building was in disarray, four significant stained-glass windows outlined the front door, gleaming in all their glory in the sunlight, in absolute contrast to the rest of the building. This had once been a church, one of three in the town. After the mill had shut down ten years before, with no work to be found, the city shrank so quickly that it no longer needed to have three churches. The church served as a soup kitchen at one time, but that was now closed. The gas plant that had opened three years ago put Boulder Ridge back on its feet and brought more people into town, but the two other churches had long since upgraded to more significant buildings, and this one had been left abandoned. Although it was ten years past its prime, and the rounded archway covered with overgrown vines and flower garden overtaken mainly by weeds, Liam could tell even now that it had once been a magnificent building.

The two rounded a corner and then another until they walked behind the old church into the back alleyway. On the other side of the alleyway was a chain-link fence for a car detailing shop and another for a mechanic shop. Other than that, there were a few dumpsters used by the businesses that backed into the alleyway and not much else.

"Look," Liam said, pointing ahead. "There's something up ahead!"

"Not something," Brynn corrected. "Someone."

Liam looked at Brynn with disbelief, "This, this is Gabe?" Liam asked, his voice breaking with concern.

.

Chapter 13

~ Gabe ~

Liam tried not to stare, as most people try not to when faced with someone who seems any less fortunate than themselves. In front of him, sitting on the ground with his back against the old church, was a man with an empty shopping cart next to him. As they got closer to the man, Liam could see his weathered face. His cheeks seemed as though they were sinking into his face, and his clothing was torn and dirty. Liam was reasonably certain that his salt and pepper, unkept hair might actually turn out to be more white than black with a wash. To Liam, he looked like a man who only marked time instead of living, and had a haunted look about him.

"Hi, Gabe!" Brynn shouted with a cheer.

"Oh, hey, kid," the man looked up at Brynn, squinting his eyes and using his hand to block the sun. Gabe did not stand up to meet her but continued, "Where have you been? I haven't seen you all week."

"This is my friend, Liam," Brynn said, nudging Liam closer to Gabe with her elbow. Gabe stretched out his dusty hand from the ground where he was still sitting. Liam felt as though not making eye contact was even more rude than staring was, so with steady eye contact, Liam reached his hand out, unsure if he was supposed to shake Gabe's hand or if he was asking for a hand up. Gabe took Liam's hand, placing his other worn and calloused hand around Liam's, and gave him a firm shake. Liam's hands clasped over Gabe's thick and knotted knuckles, holding for a moment before returning his hand to his side.

"It is nice to meet you, Gabe."

Gabe stood up; his shoulders hunched like someone who carried the weight of a hundred lifetimes. He had a kind smile, and although his eyes were sunken into his sockets, they gleamed when he spoke.

After introductions, Liam pulled Brynn aside in what he had hoped was out of earshot of Gabe, "I don't understand how you think this guy can help us," he whispered, "I know you said so, and I'm not trying to be rude, but I don't think he's really the help we're looking for."

"Try not to be so judge-y, Liam. He's seriously the smartest person I know."

Liam had never thought of himself as a judgemental person. In fact, it only made Liam sad that Gabe was obviously homeless, and he did not look down on him for it. It was not this that bothered him. It was that he was already having a hard enough time keeping up with Brynn and all her trouble. He was not sure if Gabe would add value to his mission or if he would be another person who would put Liam in uncomfortable situations. Liam thought over it for a moment but concluded that if Gabe could be of any help to him, he'd take whatever help he could get.

"How did you guys become friends, anyway?" Liam asked Brynn in another quiet whisper.

"I don't know if you've noticed this or not, Liam, but I don't exactly have a lot of friends at school. So, when I met

Gabe down here when I was skipping school one time, he let me sit with him and just talk. When I was done talking, he asked me if I wanted any advice, which I did. I'll tell you what, Liam. He gave me the best advice I'd ever gotten in my life. So, I come and visit him every once in a while, and we just hang out and talk."

Liam felt his shoulder loosen as his guard came down a little. Finally, after another long pause, he nodded in approval at Brynn.

Brynn turned back to Gabe. "Hey, Gabe, we need your help with something. We were thinking we'd take you out for some dinner and see if you could help us."

"Well, Brynn," Gabe said, stretching away from the side of the building where he was leaning, "I've never been one to turn down a BLT from the diner. And I'll help you in whatever way that I can."

Liam was surprised when he heard Gabe speak. For some reason, he thought that Gabe was likely to talk with a slur and be tripping all over himself, much like his own father, after a long day of drinking. As Gabe walked towards them, Liam noticed that he walked with a slight limp on his left side, but it was clearly from pain and not from drinking.

Gabe spoke clearly and kindly to them both, and Liam began to wonder if maybe he was more judgmental than he had thought he was. If it had not been for the way he looked, he would have seemed as every other person they passed that day.

Liam's next impression of Gabe was that he was a quiet man who seemed to spend more time listening to people than talking. He did not seem particularly wise to Liam at first, but that might have been because Brynn did so much talking that it would have been hard to get a read on anyone around while she was there. Gabe walked slowly, a slight limp in his step as he worked hard to keep up with the two as they all went.

The three walked down the street around the corner and up a couple of blocks to the diner. The diner looked like it was set in a 1950s movie, with a white exterior, bold red trim, and a bold red sign that read "Rosie's Diner." Inside, the bright red booths were offset by the black-and-white checkered flooring. As the three walked past, people stopped eating to stare. Liam felt uncomfortable, but Gabe and Brynn just walked straight to a booth and sat down.

They sat a while, to the point that Liam wondered if any of the staff had seen them sit down. But as he looked behind the counter, he saw two waitresses in red dresses and pink aprons staring at them and talking to themselves. After a short time longer, the manager joined them before walking to the booth. "Just so you know, this isn't a charity," the manager said, placing his hands on the table and gesturing to all three. However, he was very clearly looking at Gabe.

"What's that supposed to mean?" Brynn asked.

"Just that you are expected to pay for the food, so we're asking that if you don't have money, to kindly leave."

"Of course, we know we are expected to pay. Do you honestly think this is any of our first times at a diner?" Brynn sharply retorted; her eyes flashed with irritation at the assumption.

"Okay, I just wanted to let you know that our policy is to call the police anytime someone tries to skip out on the bill," the manager said again, with even more distaste in his tone.

"Well, thanks for the policy update, but you don't have to worry about that here," Brynn snapped back again.

Liam looked around, noticing that everyone in the diner was now looking at Gabe. He looked back at Gabe, who either did not see everyone staring or did not care that they were.

"Okay, thank you," said the manager, reluctantly, his harsh tone not matching his kind words, "the server will be over to take your order shortly."

The waitress was over shortly, with an eye roll and clearly in a different manner than she had with the table behind them. Gabe ordered a BLT sandwich, and Liam ordered a ham and Swiss cheese sandwich. The waitress then turned to Brynn, tapping her pen impatiently while waiting for her to order.

"What kind of steak do you have?" Brynn asked.

"All we got is the steak sandwich," the waitress groaned.

"I'll take that, please."

The waitress penned the order on her notepad. "You'd like that medium?"

"Large, if I could."

"We do medium or well done," the waitress huffed, thinking that Brynn was only trying to annoy her.

"You know what? Well done would be great. Just tell them to do the best they can, and however it comes out, will be well done enough for me."

Liam tried not to laugh at Brynn's conversation. He did not want to embarrass her, and he thought that if he had tried to correct her, it would have for sure.

The waitress stared at Brynn blankly before looking down at her notepad. "Well done," she murmured under her breath as she wrote. Then she walked away from the table to bring the order to the kitchen window.

"So, what was it that you needed my help with kids? I can't imagine that you're here just for my company."

"We just have some questions about some graffiti, hoping that maybe you've seen something like it before." Liam took the camera from his bag and went through the pictures.

"I can't say that I've seen any of these before, but I know of a place where all the artists seem to like to paint. Have you guys checked out the old train yard yet?" Gabe asked.

"We were there today," Liam answered. "We didn't find anything useful there."

"What about Graffiti Hill?" Gabe asked.

"Graffiti Hill!" Brynn shouted, snapping her finger. "Why didn't I think of that?"

"You mean to tell me that there's a hill full of graffiti called Graffiti Hill, and you just somehow forgot to mention it?"

"It's not in town, but it's not far from town,"

"I bet if you asked some of the kids that go there, something would probably point you guys in the right direction. I'm sorry. I know it's not the answer you kids were looking for, but I hope it's a start. I'd hate for you guys to buy me this dinner and not get any help from me," Gabe said.

"Oh gosh no, you are seriously the wisest person I know. I told you, Liam." Liam looked back at her as if not to say that this was probably a solution that she could have thought of on her own. "You don't believe me? Seriously, ask him anything. He basically knows everything! Watch! Gabe, what is the meaning of life?"

"I believe that the meaning of life is to live with purpose and to do it on purpose."

Brynn happily nodding her head.

"Well, that's kind of ironic, isn't it?" Liam asked, not realizing how rude his comment would sound before he said it; but was now wishing he could suck his words out of the air, where they lingered with no response.

"What do you mean, Liam?" Gabe asked, without even a tinge of anger in his voice.

"I'm sorry, I just…" Liam tripped over his own words until Gabe interrupted him.

"You think that because I'm a homeless man who spends his days living on the streets, that means that I'm not living my life with purpose?" Gabe smiled, leaning in closer to Liam, "I'll let you in on a little secret, every one of us, no matter our age, no matter where we are in life, no matter our circumstance, can live with purpose." The gravity of Gabe's words felt heavy on Liam's heart, but he also felt comfortable with them. Liam had always felt that his life had a purpose, that he had a purpose. Maybe not yet, but someday. So many people in his life told him that he was too young, that he would just amount to nothing. Once, his own father had told him that if Liam was lucky enough to end up in prison someday, that at least he could count on three square meals.

"Thank you, Gabe," Liam said. "I appreciate your wisdom."

Just as Liam had thanked Gabe, the waitress came over with three plates and passed them in front of them. Her face was still twisted into an unhappy expression. "Can I get you anything else?"

After the three shook their heads, she walked away and did not come to check on their meals again.

"I don't know about wisdom, but I'm happy to share anything that I've learned in my life."

"Learned in life?" Liam asked himself in thought, trying to think about what he had learned in his own life. Thinking about everything he had been through, all he must have learned in his life, if he took a moment to reflect from time to time, he thought maybe someday, like Gabe, he could give wise advice to some kids going through hard times.

Gabe must have guessed what was going through Liam's mind, so he continued, "When someone feels stretched thin over the coals of life, their dreams like ashes floating above themselves, it's hard to imagine that their life trials have any meaning or lessons to be learned. But I promise you, if you take the time to look back, you've learned more than you know."

Liam smiled at Gabe. His thoughts now drifted to what kind of life Gabe must have lived to be so wise, what pain and trials, triumphs and wins, and loved ones he must have lost along the way—just like Liam.

Liam's thoughts wandered until Gabe spoke again, trying to change the conversation's direction and ease Liam's busy mind. "I'll tell you what. You kids meet me tomorrow, and I'll walk with you down to Graffiti Hill. I don't like the idea of you kids walking that far from town alone. It might be a ten-minute drive, but it's a lot farther to walk."

Grateful for the offer, Liam and Brynn happily agreed.

The three had finished eating. Brynn and Liam's empty plates remained on the table, but Gabe's plate still had half his BLT sandwich. Instead of the waitress returning to take them away, the manager returned with their bill in hand. "It's time for you guys to go now. People are starting to complain."

Liam looked around, and by the look on everyone's faces and the hiss in their voices as they spoke to one another, any one of them could have complained to the manager.

"Can I get a to-go box for the rest of my sandwich, please?" Gabe asked.

The manager walked away and returned shortly with a box in hand. By the time he returned, Liam had taken the cash from his backpack and left enough to leave a ten-dollar tip.

It was dark as they exited the restaurant. The night air was cold enough that their words turned to thick fogged as they spoke. "I could give you a little more money for food tomorrow, Gabe," Liam said once they were outside and the door to the diner was closed. "You didn't have to take half of your food to go."

Gabe smiled. "You kids want to come with me? I'll show you who the sandwich is for."

Liam and Brynn followed Gabe around the corner and up a barely lit street. Gabe stopped and walked between two buildings where a woman was standing. Gabe handed her the box. "Hi, Tammy," Gabe said with a smile, "come out here, I want you to meet my friends."

The woman followed Gabe out from between the two buildings. She was tall and skinny. Her sunken cheeks and dark eyes made her look much older than she probably was. She had scabs and scars on her face, and her lips were dry and chipped.

"Hi, kids," Tammy said, placing the box on the ground beside her. She moved a lot, her hands and arms moving almost constantly.

Gabe picked the box off the ground and handed it to her again. "Make sure that you eat this, Tammy. It's from the diner, and it's great while it's still warm."

Tammy did not look at Gabe, her eyes fixed on Liam and Brynn. "These kids are so cute. My goodness, they remind me of my kids," she said, hands moving and legs almost pacing beneath her.

"You have kids?" Brynn asked, "Where are they?"

"My kids are standing in the food stamp line holding my spot for me." Tammy answered, still moving very animatedly.

"This late?" Brynn asked, "How long have they been standing there?"

"They've been there for two years now," the woman answered, her head down, swinging between her shoulders.

Without another word, Tammy stumbled back between the two buildings and disappeared into the shadows. Gabe tossed his head, directing the kids that it was time for them all to go.

The three had walked a bit in the quiet night. "Is Tammy your friend or your family?" Liam asked.

"She's just someone I met out here," Gabe answered. "She's been going through a hard time, and we all have to stick together out here. It can be dangerous."

Liam nodded in understanding and did not ask for anything more.

"This is where I'll stop," Gabe said, stopping in front of a back-alley entrance. Liam looked down the dark road, shadowed by the street lights and the large buildings on each side. Liam tried to focus his eyes to adjust for the lack of light, but he was pretty sure he could just make out the outlines of a large cardboard box on the ground at the other end of the alley. Liam imagined this was probably where Gabe spent his nights, and his heart sank at the thought.

"We'll see you tomorrow then, Gabe," Liam said. "Thank you for your help."

"Meet me at the church in the morning. We'll walk out to Graffiti Hill together." With that, Gabe said goodnight, walked down the dark alley, and was gone from Liam's sight.

Liam and Brynn had walked together down the road a bit further from where Gabe had stopped before either of them spoke again. "So, Liam, have you thought about where you're going to be sleeping tonight?" Brynn asked, pointing out what was an obvious question to her.

Liam stopped walking momentarily, realizing that the thought had not even crossed his mind. "I had honestly been so wrapped up in everything I guess I hadn't even thought about it."

"Well," Brynn looked like she was thinking over clearly what she would say next. "I'm not allowed to have friends in my house, but I can sneak you into the shed in the backyard if you're okay sleeping there. It has a heater in it, so it should be warm enough, and there's an old couch in there. It probably smells like cigarettes, but it's comfy. Just promise me you won't touch anything. My parents are super paranoid and will seriously know if anything is moved."

Liam nodded. Although the idea of sleeping in Brynn's shed was not ideal, it was better than any plan that came to Liam at that moment. Brynn and Liam continued to walk down the street they were on until they turned down the next block onto a dimly lit street, with one light for the entire block. They walked past four or five houses until Brynn turned into a driveway and approached the backyard gate. The house was small, and even in the faint light, Liam could see that it was run-down. Along the side of the house, the blue paint on the wooden siding was faded and peeling from years of the hot sun beating against it, the gutters that stretched across the roof were warped and falling over the front door, and most of the front windows were covered with tin foil.

As the two approached the house, Brynn glanced back to Liam, holding her finger against her lip, and spoke in a hushed whisper: "We'll sneak around the back to the shed, but we had to be quiet. My parents will freak out if they see you."

Together, they walked along the gravel driveway down the side of the house, ducking under the open window where they could hear the TV from inside but heard no one. Behind the house was a fenced backyard, and once through the side gate was a stone path that led to a large shed. The grass in the backyard was long and unkempt, and the patio that stretched from the back of the house had a slight lean and was missing some stairs. The shed looked better than the house, and Liam was sure it was more of a shop than a shed.

Brynn quietly opened the left side of the double door and motioned Liam inside.

"I'll have to lock the door behind you, or it won't shut, but I'll come out and get you as soon as I get up!" Brynn closed the door after saying goodnight, and Liam could hear her footsteps until they were just shuffles quieting in the distance, and then there was nothing.

Liam turned away from the door and stood in the darkness. Brynn must have turned the backyard light on because suddenly, there was enough light that Liam could see a little more than just the surrounding shadows.
As Liam's eyes adjusted to what little light he had, he scanned the room. He tried to ignore the spider webs along the ceiling and the cold, damp floor that touched his socked feet as he took off his shoes at the door. To his right, he could see a stack of empty beer bottles, most in a garbage can to his left, but it was so packed that cans and bottles were spilled over and were covering the surrounding floor.

"Don't trip over those bottles and alert the entire town that you're in here," Liam instructed himself in almost a song.

In the middle of the room was the couch, with cigarette burn holes and stained by the years it had been spent used as a smoking seat. In front of the sofa sat a coffee table with discolored rings on it, stained from old drinks that had once sat there, and Liam soon realized it was wobbly when he tried to place his backpack onto it. Liam thought he'd get used to the smell faster, but the stench of mildew and old cigarettes was the kind of smell that Liam felt as it clung to his clothes, hair, and skin.

Beside the coffee table was the heater that Brynn had told him would be there. Liam plugged it into the extension cord beside it and turned the switch on, but nothing happened. Liam tried to unplug it, hoping it would turn on with a second try. But again, nothing happened. Liam followed the extension cord along the floor and up the back wall where it was plugged in. He unplugged the extension cord and plugged it back in, but the heater did not turn on. "Okay," Liam said to himself, pulling an extra pair of socks out of his backpack. "It's going to be a chilly night."

Liam unplugged the heater from the extension cord to leave it as he had found it and made his way carefully over to the couch, making sure not to make any noise that might be loud enough to reach the house. Liam took off his jacket, quietly placing it on the floor. The pocket contents raddled as it dropped, and the noise reminded Liam of the heavy necklace and cash weighing in the pocket. "I have to make sure to take that back to the pawn shop first thing tomorrow," Liam thought. He went to the couch and tried to settle in for the night.

Chapter 14

~ Unrested Refuge ~

Liam sat on the couch, nearly sinking to the floor, and realized that the couch was holding most of the smell filling the room. He was excited to find a thick wool blanket draping down the back of the couch. He unraveled the blanket and then bunched his backpack up to try to use it as a pillow, first pulling out the envelope and camera from the front pocket and placing them on top of his jacket. As Liam laid down on his side, his head sunk deep into the couch, the weight on the second cushion lifting the lower half of his body above his head, twisting his back unnaturally, and with each breath he took, he felt like the wind was being kicked from his lungs. Liam thought about Gabe as he lay there, wondering what kind of sleep he could have in that cold back alley in a cardboard box and with that thought, Liam's home away from home did not seem so bad, and he laid his head deeper into the couch and closed his eyes.

Liam was weary down to his bones, so much so that moving from side to side or lifting his heavy arms to get more comfortable seemed impossible. Liam wrapped his arms around himself, trying to preserve any heat in his body. The night stretched on, and although Liam was beyond exhausted from only sleeping a few hours in the past few days, he tossed on the hard couch for hours, sleepless as the night drifted along, hour after hour.

Dogs barked, and the sound of car alarms sounding nearby seemed to keep Liam on high alert as he lay with wide-open eyes, watching the frost as it settled on the outside of the window. Liam shivered and tried to hide his nose in his shirt to keep warm. Liam switched sides on the couch, hoping to get more comfortable. He laid back down and pulled the thick wool blanket to his chin. The thick blanket was neither soft nor as warm as Liam thought it would be, and the wool felt like straw against his bare arms and neck.

Liam tried to lay as still as possible because every time he adjusted his position on the couch, the blanket would scratch his skin, and a new cloud of ash and dust would stir into the air, settling on Liam, filling his nose and parching his mouth.

Finally, day broke, and the sun came through the shed's cracked window, distorting the light against Liam's face. Liam's eyes were still closed, but the light burned his tired eyes through his heavy eyelids. He tried to cover them with his arm and recover a little more sleep. Liam could hear footsteps drawing closer through the backyard grass and then up the stone path until they were just outside the shed door. His eyes opened on high alert, and he sat up on the couch as quickly as his sore back and ribs would allow. Liam had half a mind to hide. As he sat at the edge of the couch, he listened for any sound outside the door.

"Knock, knock, knock," Liam heard a familiar voice say, much to his relief, accompanied by a firm knock on the door panel. "Are you awake?"

"I am now," Liam replied, sighing in relief as he hung his head in his hands and ran his fingers through his hair. He stayed sitting on the couch, waiting for the door to open.

Knock, knock, knock went the door again, "are you even alive in here?"

Brynn slowly opened the door, peering her head through.

"I am. Didn't you hear me say that I was awake?"

"I heard some mumbles coming from your side of the door, but I had no idea if you were saying yes or no!" Brynn smirked.

Liam laughed, "You weren't sure if I was saying yes or no to being awake?" He rubbed his eyes, scratching even more dust into his red-veined, dry eyes. "What time is it?"

"It's just about nine," Brynn replied, walking over to the couch. "Jeesh, it sure doesn't look like you had a good sleep. Were you too warm out here? That heater can get too hot sometimes."

"I wish that heater got too hot," Liam laughed. "It doesn't even turn on."

"Oh," Brynn said, walking over to the heater and plugging it in. The heater did not turn on, but when Brynn gave it a quick kick, it fired up without issue. "Ah, there you go!" Brynn said with a sense of pride.

"Thanks," Liam laughed, warming his hands next to the heater.

"So, it must have been a cold night."

"It was pretty cold in here for sure," Liam confirmed.

"Well, if it makes you feel any better, it isn't much better inside," Brynn remarked. "Come on though, we have to sneak out of here before my parents wake up."

Liam quickly tidied up where he had attempted to sleep, unplugged the heater, folded the blanket, draped it back over the side of the couch, grabbed his jacket, placed the envelope and camera back into his backpack, and followed her.

"Before we meet up with Gabe and head out of town, we need to drop this necklace and cash back off at the pawnshop," Liam said after he stretched his arms through his jacket and zipping it closed up to his chin and securely hanging his bag against his back, "there's no way I'm walking around town with these stolen goods in my jacket pocket."

"We'll do it later. The pawn shop is on the other side of town from where we're meeting Gabe."

"No, there's no way," Liam shook his head. "It sure sounds like you don't even want to return the stuff!"

"No, I promise we will, but we can't waste any more time. We'll be late heading out to Graffiti Hill, and we won't even get there until dark!"

"That's fine. I have a flashlight in my backpack. We're going to the pawn shop first!" Liam scrapped his finger against his teeth. "Before we go, though, I need to use that bathroom, brush my teeth, and have a giant glass of water!"

"No way! I already told you my parents don't let me have people over. They would seriously flip a brick if they saw you!"

"They won't see me, I promise!" Liam insisted.

Brynn stared at Liam, the twist in her mouth indicating that she was annoyed at his persistence. "Okay, okay. We do have a bathroom just off the boot room. You can use it quickly, but you can't go in the house any further than that. And you have to be silent!"

Liam laughed, thinking that the seriousness in Brynn's face and tone was an exaggeration for some comedic effect.

"I'm serious, Liam. You can't wake them up!"

Liam nodded his head in agreement, realizing that Brynn was serious. Walking up to the porch door, Brynn looked at Liam with a serious look, the narrowing of her eyes screaming in reiteration to him that he needed to be quiet. Brynn opened a back door that led into the house from the backyard, and once Liam was through the door, she carefully closed it again.

"The bathroom is right there. Get in, get out, and hurry up!"

Liam looked inside the bathroom door, the room hardly big enough to go inside and turn around.

"I'll be right out here waiting for you. Seriously, hurry up!" Brynn said again in a hoarse whisper.

Liam went inside and closed the door. He used the toilet, washed his hands, and brushed his teeth. Running the water for a moment to let it get warm enough to wash his face with, Liam looked into the mirror above the sink, hardly recognizing the sleep-deprived, red-eyed boy who was looking back at him. His skin looked cold, waxy and pale. His eyes half closed despite him trying to open them wider as he stared at himself. Liam ran the water onto his hands to check the temperature, pooling it into his hand and splashing it across his face a few times.

Liam shut off the faucet as he heard movement above his head. The sound of heavy steps walking across the floor above him grew louder and closer. Liam opened the door slowly, but it was too late. Outside the door stood a thin, dark-haired woman speaking to Brynn in the next doorway down the hall, which connected the porch to the rest of the house. Quickly, Liam pulled the door, not fully closing it, fearing that it would be loud enough to be heard. Then he turned off the light. Liam could still hear walking above him, and he made himself as flat as he could against the bathroom wall, but he was sure that the sound of his own breathing was loud enough to shake the house.

Liam could not hear the conversation between Brynn and who he presumed was her mom. He pulled the door open to the slight crack, and with one eye peaking through, Liam watched them, hoping that Brynn would give him a sign or an opening to sneak out the door undetected.

The thin woman seemed to speak harshly to Brynn while moving her hands around dramatically. He could hear the heavy footsteps walking down the stairs, and he could feel a bead of sweat as it fell off his head and ran down his brow and nose.

"Oh, you know that Phil loves you, Brynn," her mother said. "If he didn't care about you, he wouldn't put this roof over our heads. I don't think it's too much for him to ask for simple things like you remembering to lock the door when you come home."

"Okay mom. Now come over here mom," Brynn spoke unnaturally loudly, "I want to show you something I noticed last night."

Brynn and her mother walked out of sight. Their voices fell to a quiet mumble. Liam sprang the door open quietly and went out the back door, all without making a sound. After a few minutes, Brynn followed out the side door. Liam was so quiet about leaving that Brynn was not sure if he had moved from the bathroom.

"Liam!" Brynn called out, not quite in a yell.

"Over here!" he answered.

Brynn found Liam sitting against the fence that separated the backyard from the back alley. Brynn stared at Liam, his face pale, like all the blood had been scared out of it.

"Phew! That was close!" Brynn laughed, holding her hand out to Liam to help him up.

Liam did not laugh back. The gravity of Brynn's warnings about going into the house had not been lost on him, and although he still did not know exactly what she meant when she had warned him about what her parents' reaction would have been if they had found him there, he was still visibly shaking.

"Okay," Brynn started, trying to ease Liam's nerves. "Let's go find Gabe!"

"Not until we return these to the pawn shop!" Liam said after he had found his voice again, patting his jacket pocket.

Brynn rolled her eyes. "Right, let's go!"

Most of the back alley was still blanketed with a light frost, hidden from the sun between the rows of houses, not yet touched by its heat. Walking down the path was not easy.

The road was trenched with deep pits down the middle of the gravel road, left by the giant tires on Brynn's neighbor's truck. The two walked along the side of the road, the frosted grass snapping under their steps. They continued on, pushing past thick branches against the fence lines and dodging under low-hanging branches from overhead trees as they went. Dogs lined against the fences, barking and growling at Liam and Brynn as they walked by.

Finally, they reached the pavement on the other side of the alleyway, and from there, they walked straight down to the main road. The pawn shop was just a few blocks up, then a block left off the main road, on one of the many roads that made up the town center. It was busy, especially leaving the relatively quiet of the residential area. There were baby boutiques, clothing shops, and even a pet shop all lined up along the same road, and on the far end and around a corner was Patty's Pawn Shop.

Liam and Brynn reached the end of the block, where Brynn suddenly stopped outside the glass front door of a gas station on the corner leading to Patty's Pawnshop, which was just out of sight.

"Let's run into the gas station first and grab some snacks and water for our road trip," Brynn suggested. "Then we can use the grocery bag to put the necklace and cash in when we hang it on the door of Patty's."

Liam was unsure if Brynn was stalling, but reluctantly, he agreed and followed Brynn inside the gas station. The gas station reminded Liam of Mr. Lister's convenience store, minus the comfort of his happy friend behind the counter. The man behind the counter did not even look up to greet them. He was too focused on some magazine he was reading to notice them. The two gathered their goods for their walk. Brynn grabbed a few sandwiches and a handful of different kinds of chocolate bars while Liam reached into the fridge and grabbed three bottles of cold water. As they walked to the counter to pay, Liam could not shake the feeling that someone was watching him. Liam took his backpack off his shoulder, and while he did so, from the corner of his eye, he was sure that he could see someone staring at him. He glanced back, trying not to be too obvious. As he did, the kid quickly turned their eyes away.

"Do you know that kid over there?" Liam whispered to Brynn, slightly nudging his head behind him. "He's staring at me."

But before Brynn noticed who Liam was even talking about, something caught her eye. Panicked, she started elbowing Liam aggressively in his side, "Liam!"

Chapter 15

~Faith in Friendships Restored~

"Liam!" Brynn shouted, "Look! Is that you?"

Brynn was pointing to a television above the counter. There was no sound coming from the it, but it was airing a local news station. Overtaking the entire screen was Liam's picture with big, bold letters across the bottom that read "MISSING."

"My brother must have reported me missing!" Liam suddenly felt all too aware of how many people were around him. He pulled the hood of his sweater to cover his face as much as he could, feeling a cool bead of sweat fall down his neck. The screen flashed back to the reporter, and Liam felt some sense of relief that his picture was gone. He tapped his foot anxiously as he waited for the customer in front of them to collect their change from the counter. He rushed to the counter at his first opportunity, trying to be quick but not to bring any attention to himself. Then a thought came to him; leaning over to Brynn, he whispered into her ear.

"You don't think my brother would have hired a private investigator to find me, do you? Because that person behind me is definitely still staring at me."

Brynn looked over her shoulder. The young man behind her was tall but looked no older than eighteen or so and wore a mean look on his face. He wore a black sweater and had dark eyes that were still fixated on Liam. Brynn shook her head, "He doesn't look old enough to be a private investigator," she said this with such confidence Liam did not even think about the fact that she probably had no idea how old private investigators were. "I've never seen him. You don't know him?" she asked. "He is definitely staring at you."

"I've never seen him before either," Liam answered. Liam looked over his shoulder one last time, and from the corner of his eye, he could see the guy still staring at him unwaveringly. A shiver went down Liam's spine, and he turned back to the cash register. The cashier rang through all of their items and bagged them. As quickly as Liam could, he counted out his cash for the payment, "keep the change," he said, and they were out the door in a hurry.

"We'll have to keep a pretty low profile now, Liam," Brynn said once they were outside. "You're a wanted man now!"

Liam laughed at the ridiculousness of Brynn's comment, but it did not calm his nerves. Liam looked around cautiously. He still felt like someone was watching him, but he did not see the stranger from the store anywhere. He swallowed hard to choke down his nerves. He had other things to worry about at the moment.

"Okay, we've got your stuff, now let's just drop this stuff off," Liam said, patting his heavy jacket pocket where the necklace and cash were held. "And then we can be off to Graffiti Hill."

Liam handed Brynn the bag with their snacks and water in it. Brynn knelt down on the cold asphalt, emptied the contents into her backpack, and gave Liam the bag.

"Here," Brynn said, "you can put the necklace and stuff in here, so we can just hang it inside the door."

Liam took the necklace and cash from his pocket and put them into the grocery bag, and then placed the bag into his backpack and zipped it closed. Liam stood up and was about to ask Brynn which direction they were heading in when he felt a violent tug on his backpack which was still in his hand. Liam tightened his grip as quickly as possible, but it was too late. Liam was knocked to the ground as the thief ran by them, and he took off down the road.

"That's him!" Liam cried from the ground, scrambling to his feet. "That's who was inside the gas station staring at me!"

Brynn helped Liam to his feet. "What do we do? Call the police?" Liam asked.

"No! Are you crazy? Unless you want to be the one to explain to the police that the stolen backpack was full of stolen items! Besides, aren't you forgetting…Wanted man?"

"Well, what do we do?" Liam asked again.

"We'll have to catch him! Let's go!"

With that, Brynn was gone, chasing after the kid and Liam's backpack. A few steps behind, Liam chased after the two, who had now rounded a corner and were out of sight.

Liam caught up to Brynn, who shouted at him, "I'll chase him down this alley. You go that way, and we'll cut him off at the corner!"

Liam turned down the next road to do as Brynn had said, leaving her chasing the kid down the alleyway. When Liam reached the corner where he had expected to catch them, the alleyway was silent, and they were gone. Liam ran to the end of that block, looking both ways, but he could not see Brynn or the thief. Liam paused for a moment, not knowing which direction to run. After some thinking, Liam decided to take the road leading left, and when he did, he was scanning the road for any indication that he was running the right way.

Liam lost his breath, feeling that his lungs had caught on fire. He stopped running, and his legs went numb and collapsed under him. Liam sat on the sidewalk. He had run at least five blocks, possibly in the wrong direction. He sat for a while, without any idea of where Brynn was or his backpack that had not only the items that Brynn had taken from the pawnshop that they were about to return, but in his backpack was also his cash and camera but most importantly to Liam, the letter from Jacob, still sealed in the envelope in the front pocket.

Once Liam had caught his breath again, he stood up. His legs felt like jello as they struggled to lift him to his feet. He looked up and down the streets around him but still could not see anything. He was sure his backpack was gone forever and was unsure how he would find Brynn. Liam looked in every direction, still seeing nothing to help him pick up his chase again. Liam decided to trace his steps back to the gas station, hoping that when Brynn had given up the chase, she would also head back there.

When Liam returned to the gas station, and went inside to look for Brynn, but she was not there. Liam came out to the sidewalk and sat down against the building, pulling his knees to his chest and placing his head on his folded arms. He wanted to cry, and he probably would have if he had not been so exhausted from his failed chase. Liam sat unmoved for what felt like a lifetime. Each moment that passed, he felt any sliver of hope passing away with it.

Brynn was probably gone, realizing that the fun was over without the backpack and the letter, and Liam had failed at the only thing he'd ever tried to do. Just as he was about to stand, he heard the "thunk" of something heavy being dropped beside him. He looked over, and his missing backpack was sitting beside him, tattered and dirty. Standing beside him was Brynn, sweaty and out of breath.

Liam grabbed it and jumped to his feet.

"I'm not sure how you think a chase works, but it doesn't work well when you're just sitting there!" Brynn laughed.

Liam grabbed Brynn by both shoulders and pulled her in for a hug.

"Thank you so much! How did you do it?" Liam had now let go of Brynn, securely placed his backpack onto his back, and tightened the straps.

"Do you really want to know?" Brynn laughed.

"Who was he?" Liam asked.

"He didn't say, but I don't think he was after you, just your backpack once he saw that you had cash in it," Brynn answered.

"I can't believe you did that for me," Liam said, placing the backpack tightly on his shoulders.

"Of course I did! What are friends for!" Brynn smiled back at Liam. "Now can we please get these things to Patty's so we can go?"

Liam and Brynn left the sidewalk outside the gas station, walking towards the corner where the pawnshop was.

"I'm just going to quickly open the door, hang the bag on the door handle, and leave. Get ready to run, and that'll be that!"

"I'll be ready for sure!" Brynn confirmed, "But how is she even going to know that you hung it on the door handle? What if someone else just takes it off the door handle and steals it? Then is that really any better than me taking it?

"Okay, fine," Liam said, "I'll hang it on the door and then knock really loud so she'll come and look and find it. I don't know, maybe I'll call her name or something. I'll figure it out, but let's just get this done."

Liam and Brynn rounded the corner, and Liam felt his neck strangle as Brynn pulled him back around by the back of his shirt collar. Liam took a moment, stumbling on his feet before landing beside Brynn.

"What?" Liam cried out, rubbing his sore neck with his hand.

"Shhh!" Brynn hushed, hugging the side of the building. She and Liam peered beyond the corner of the building to the next street in front of the pawn shop.

"Is that Officer Douglas talking to Patty?" Liam asked Brynn, dashing behind the corner. "Does this town only have one cop?"

"It's a small town, and that's definitely Officer Douglas talking to Patty. And she's definitely giving him a statement."

Liam felt his stomach suddenly go cold, as he swallowed over the lump in his dry throat. He tried to take deep breaths, trying to calm his racing heart as he lay against the brick building. Brynn was still peering around the corner, looking back to Liam occasionally to ensure he had not passed out. Liam lifted himself from the building, scraping his shoulder against the rough surface, trying to stick as close as he could and out of sight as he joined Brynn, who was trying to overhear any part of the conversation she could.

"We'll just have to figure out another way to do this," Liam said.

"Do this? Are you kidding me? You and your conscience are always getting in the way. If we could just eliminate your conscience altogether, we'd probably have found your mystery person and delivered that letter already!"

Liam felt annoyed, as if it was his conscience that had gotten them into this mess to begin with.

Officer Douglas and Patty spoke for a while, the officer taking notes on a notepad and giving Patty the occasional nod, but Liam and Brynn could hear nothing of what they said. After he closed his notepad, clicked his pen closed, and placed them both into his front pocket, he said a few more words to Patty before she walked back into her shop and he started to walk off.

"He's walking over this way!" Brynn whispered to Liam. "We need to hide!"

They looked around, scrambling over each other, their eyes dashing back and forth along the street, looking for anywhere to hide.

"Over here!" Liam called to Brynn, looking in the box of a red pickup truck full of flattened cardboard.

They climbed over the tailgate and laid inside of the truck's box, covering themselves with a cardboard blanket. They could hear Officer Douglas approaching—first, the jingling of his handcuffs hitting against each other, then him speaking into the radio on his shoulder.

"This is Officer Douglas. I just left Patty's Pawnshop. There are no security cameras, but I got a description of the suspects—just a couple of kids. I'm going to canvas the area to see if there were any more thefts that haven't been reported."

Brynn and Liam lifted their heads enough to see Officer Douglas stopped at the hardware store next to the parked truck. Officer Douglas took out his notepad, flipping through the pages from his conversation with Patty, taking a few glances around occasionally. Just as Officer Douglas closed his notepad and put it back into his pocket, there was an elderly man struggling to push the door of the hardware store open, trudging in labored steps, carrying what seemed like a heavy box in his arms. The old man nodded behind the package to the officer, and Officer Douglas nodded back and stepped towards him.

"That looks a bit heavy," Officer Douglas called to the old man, reaching out his arms to take the box. "Here, let me give you a hand."

The old man unloaded his arms into Officer Douglas' hands, "Thank you very much. It was getting heavier with each step."

Officer Douglas let out a laugh. "Where are you parked?"

"Just over here," replied the old man, walking across the sidewalk and then leaning against his red pickup truck. "This truck right here."

"Do you want this in the box or the backseat?"

"Oh, just the backseat is fine," the old man hurried around, opening the truck door and closing it again once Officer Douglas had dropped the box on the seat.

"I really must thank you. Now, if only I could bring you home to unload it for me, too!" The old man chuckled.

"I wish I could help you out there, but duty calls."

The old man laid his open hand on the officer's shoulder, padding it gently with a smile building across his face. "I can imagine it does. My son is a police officer over in Boundary. He's always sharing stories with me about his work. But I thought this was a safe side of town. Is there anything the general public needs to be worried about?"

"Oh, nothing you have to worry about; just a couple of kids took some goods from a store up the road. But not to worry, we'll catch them in no time, I assure you," Officer Douglas stood high in his shoes, looking over the side of the box of the truck. Liam and Brynn held their breath so that nothing moved. "That's a lot of recycling you've got in the box there," Officer Douglas said, looking into the box of the truck.

"Oh, my grandson likes to use them as race car tracks for his toy cars. It's convenient for me and saves me the trip to the depot. Well, thank you again, officer. I'll let you get back to your day."

Officer Douglas nodded as the old man got into the parked truck, starting it up in a roar.

"Liam, we have a problem!"

Liam and Brynn laid without moving, still hidden beneath the cardboard as the truck drove away. They could hear the elderly man's music playing through the open window, which sounded like it was from a radio station that was at least a hundred years old. The old man did not notice them and was humming along to his music. They waited until they were a few blocks before they sat up.

"What do we do now?" Liam asked Brynn, who was sitting up enough to see Liam but still low enough to not be seen by approaching traffic.

"I have no idea. But hey, at least we're sitting in the back of some old man's truck and not the back of Officer Douglas' cruiser," Brynn laughed. "I think we just wait it out a few more blocks so we know for sure that we're far enough away from him and that pawn shop," Brynn insisted.

"Well, we'll have to find time to make it back there, maybe after it gets dark, and the store is closed or something."

"Back where?" Brynn asked. "The pawnshop? As if! I'm not going back there!"

"Brynn…."

"Listen, Liam, I respect that you want to do the right thing, blah blah, and we tried to! So that has to count for something!"

"No, we have to, or I'll just go back myself and do it!"

Brynn shook her head, but did not bother to counter his argument. "One predicament at a time," she insisted. "Let's start by figuring out how we're going to get out of the back of this truck first. I'd say we've driven at least six or seven blocks by now. But with all this arguing, I just realized that we've been driving in the opposite direction that you and I need to be going in, so if we don't jump out of here pretty soon, we might as well not bother walking out to Graffiti Hill today."

"Well, maybe at the next stop sign, we just jump out," Liam suggested.

"Seems simple enough, but we'll have to be quick. Most people don't even bother with a rolling stop at stop signs."

The two uncovered themselves and laid flat on top of the cardboard until they heard the brakes grinding as the truck slowed to a stop. Quickly, they sat up, hanging their legs over the right side of the truck and jumping down to the pavement, scurrying to the sidewalk as quickly as possible.

"Do you think he heard us?" Liam asked

"No, he's too busy listening to the music that he rescued from the nineteen twenties. I'm not even sure which was worse, the cardboard pushing my head into the metal or that man's taste in music!"

Liam looked around, scanning the streets and buildings around him. Although just a short drive away, the place he was looked different from where the pawnshop was. It was busier, and the buildings were fancier and taller. "So, how far away are we from where we told Gabe we'd meet him?"

"Well, since we have to circle back and around at least ten blocks to where the pawnshop is to avoid any chance of running into Officer Douglas, I'd say we have at least fifteen blocks to walk just to get to where we told him we'd meet him."

Liam and Brynn began circling back, staying off the main roads and sticking to as many back alleyways as possible. After walking for about an hour, Liam looked ahead and noticed the old church where they had met Gabe the day before. They went around the back of the building, but there was no one there.

"I don't get it," Brynn said. "This is where he told us to meet him."

"Well, maybe he changed his mind about going out there with us," Liam wondered.

"No, I don't think he would do that," Brynn assured.

"Well, we don't have time to wait here for him if we plan to get there and back before it gets dark. Do you know how to get to Graffiti Hill?"

"Of course I do," Brynn said. "Can we please wait for Gabe for five minutes? If he isn't here in five minutes, we can just leave."

Liam agreed.

"Maybe he's on the other side of the building," Brynn said as she walked along the other side of the church. She was only gone for a few seconds before she walked back, shaking her head. "He's not on that side. Did you see anyone sitting out front when we walked up?"

"No," Liam shook his head.

Five minutes had passed, and there was still no sign of Gabe. Brynn begged for another minute, but after three more, she agreed to leave without him.

Chapter 16

~Delving into Despair for~

Answers

The two had walked from the busy center of town to an area surrounded by quiet walking paths and dog parks, then past the residential area of town. Now, they had finally reached the edge of town at an intersection separated by an overhead traffic light. It was half past four o'clock, and their unexpected delays had them leaving town much later than they had meant to. One road was the highway leading out of town, and the other was a dangerous goods route that led around. Liam and Brynn stood at the intersection of the two, waiting for the lights to change so they could cross.

"Now we just have to cross at the lights here and head down the dangerous goods route for a bit; Graffiti Hill is a way up a back road," Brynn said.

The road seemed to shake as the giant trucks hauling their trailers sped by them, using the bypass to get around the town with their goods. As the lights changed, the two crossed the road and walked down the bypass briefly before turning down a gravel road. The road ahead stretched as far as Liam's sight could reach, with dips and hills and rounding corners as it went. Dirt kicked up in a cloud behind their feet with every step as they walked along the gravel road. The sound of birds calling echoed in the open sky as they headed south for winter. At times, the clouds shadowed parts of the sun that sat at half-mast. Lined on each side of the narrow road were deep trenches carved out by the water from melted snow in spring that drained down each side but had now long dried up in the summer heat. Above the ditches were fields and more fields with scattered bales of hay, and as they grew more and more distant, the fields looked like yellow and orange patchwork, quilted together. There were farmhouses, few and far between, with smoke billowing from their chimneys before gently settling on the skyline in the distance. Beyond those fields were hills that seemed like shadows beneath the painted blue sky, which was clear, with the exception of one or two big marshmallow clouds drifting lazily over them.

On his right, Liam could see the highway in the short distance, running parallel to the dirt road they were walking on, separated by a line of large fields. The highway was far enough away that Liam knew he would not have to worry about any passing police officers recognizing them while driving by, but close enough that he was sure that they would be able to spot any police cruiser driving along it.

A light wind was coming in from the west, pouring over them and sweeping through the trees, and taking with it what was left of the leaves that clung to them and leaving the few trees along the roadside barren. Liam and Brynn covered their eyes, lifting their hoods over their heads to block them from the dirt that was now stirred up on the road.

As they rounded their first corner, the wind seemed to hold on to the fields and away from them. Liam looked up to see a strange figure on the road ahead. "I see someone! Just up the road!"

Brynn lifted her head from under her hood. "I see them too!"

"Should we hide?" Liam asked, unsure how he felt about meeting a stranger on a back road.

"Do you think that they saw us? They might be far enough away that they won't see us," Brynn answered. "Let's just try to keep our distance for now. It might just be a farmer from one of those houses up there. I'm sure they'll just turn off at one of those driveways coming up."

The two continued to walk, and although they tried to keep a distance between themselves and the stranger on the road ahead, the gap was slowly closing when Brynn announced, "That's Gabe!" as she ran to catch up to him.

Brynn called out to Gabe, trying to ensure she did not startle him.

"Oh, I'm glad to see you kids. When you didn't show up at the church, I thought I'd be meeting you there. I didn't think for a second that I was ahead of you on the road."

"Yeah, sorry," Brynn said. "We had a little fuzz delay!"

Although Liam could not put it into words, he felt a certain peace as they continued their walk with Gabe. There was something so steady about Gabe, something so steadfast that he had never felt in his life, and it gave Liam a sense of security. Liam walked between Gabe and Brynn down the gravel road, and had Brynn chatting off like a songbird in one ear. Liam realized that Gabe spent more time listening and only spoke when asked a question, which worked out nicely for Brynn because asking Gabe questions was one of her favourite ways to pass the time.

"I've got a new question for you, Gabe!" Brynn began. "What is the best advice you've ever gotten?" Brynn asked, shuffling her feet in the gravel rocks on the road.

"The best advice I've ever gotten?" Gabe repeated back to her, closing his left eye and turning his head up in reflection. He paused another moment in thought before he answered, "My father once told me to never take criticism from someone you wouldn't ask advice from."

"Good stuff, good stuff," Brynn nodded in approval like she was drinking up all of Gabe's wisdom. Brynn then turned to Liam. "Ask him something, Liam," she said, nudging him with her elbow.

"What?" Liam asked. He was utterly content to just listen to Brynn ask the questions. "I have no idea what to ask.

You just go ahead. I'd rather listen. If I think of anything, I'll ask him."

Brynn waved her hand dismissively. "Just ask him anything!"

"Sure," Liam smiled at Brynn's persistence and then turned to Gabe. "Can I ask you something, Gabe?" He said, somewhat sarcastically, trying to humor Brynn.

"Of course, Liam, ask me anything," Gabe smiled.

Liam thought about it for a while, but no questions came to mind. He glanced back at Brynn, her eyes wide with anticipation as she was impatiently waiting for him to ask Gabe something, anything. Liam looked back at Gabe. "Umm…" he stalled. "Why do we drive on a parkway and park in a driveway?"

"Are you serious, Liam?" Brynn sounded almost insulted by the question. "You can ask him anything, and that's what you ask? Ask him about life, his best philosophies about anything, but it has to be something real!"

Gabe laughed. "Brynn, he doesn't have to ask me anything if he doesn't want to. Not everyone likes to play this game like you do."

"Yes, he does!" she insisted. "Ask him something better than that, Liam."

Liam thought it about for another moment. There was something that he wanted to ask Gabe, something he had been wondering about. He drew in a deep breath through his nose, looking down the road ahead. "Why do you think people take their own lives?"

Gabe looked at Liam, and Liam sensed worry across his face as he asked, "Let me ask you this first, Liam, before I answer. Why do you ask?"

Brynn spoke up before Liam had the chance to answer. "His brother took his own life a few days ago."

Liam looked at Brynn sharply. Liam felt a flood of mixed emotions take over him. One moment, he felt angry that she felt comfortable enough talking about his brother's death so casually. But in the next heartbeat of a second, he was grateful that she had said it, so he did not have to.

The three walked quietly until Gabe spoke. "I'm sorry, Liam, that you are having to go through that. That is a lot for anyone, but more so for someone so young. There are so many reasons why someone might take their life, but I think what you're feeling is what my therapist from the military would have called 'survivors' guilt'."

Liam turned the phrase in his head before asking what it meant.

"Survivors' guilt is like carrying an emotional weight because you've made it through a difficult time or traumatic event where someone else did not," Gabe said, pulling a deep breath in before continuing. "It's feeling guilty for being alive when others aren't, and it makes you wonder why you're still here and they aren't. It really is more than that." Gabe paused, thinking over what he was trying to say. "It's a complex mix of emotions. It's sadness, shame, and confusion, and it sounds strange, but it's completely normal to feel the way you are."

Liam felt like Gabe had just lifted a weight off his young, weight-barren shoulders. Finally, there was someone who really did understand what he was feeling and going through. He steadied his breathing, trying not to cry. "The kids at my school said he took the easy way out."

"I've held a loaded gun to my head; believe me, Liam, that isn't easy." Gabe put his hand on Liam's shoulder. "I'm so sorry this happened. This should never have happened."

Liam's closed his eyes, as tears streamed down his face.

"As for your question, Liam, people take their own lives because they lose hope. Life without hope gets to be too much; they feel like a burden to everyone around them and feel like this is the only way out. I'll use a story as an example. I used to be involved in a support group where I saw people fighting through their depression. It wasn't a large group, only about ten of us or so. We'd get together and talk about our week, check in with each other, that sort of thing. There was a man who'd show up every week and sit in the back of the room. He was quiet, and did not say much. He was depressed and getting better; at least, that's what he told all of us. One week, he didn't show up for our meeting, and we all wondered where he was, but it wasn't until the second missed meeting that I began to worry. I got his address from our group files and went to his house to check on him. I remember walking up to his door and knocking on it, fully expecting to see him open the door and tell me that he just had a lot of things going on, and that's why he wasn't able to make it to the meetings."

"Is that what happened? Did he answer the door?" Liam asked.

"No, he didn't answer the door. His widow did, with tears in her eyes, as she told me that her husband had taken his own life the week before. I told everyone when I went to the support group the following week. Everyone began crying. We were crying for him and his family. We all put whatever money we could together to help with his funeral, and I brought it to his wife the next day. That night, when I got back to where I was staying, I couldn't stop thinking about the heartbreak of that woman, and that's the day I realized what depression really is. It's a thief, and it's a liar. It tricks you into believing your friends and family are better off without you. But when I stood in front of his grieving wife or at the support group full of grieving people, I did wonder why he didn't reach out to us if he was hurting so badly, while there was still a chance for us to help him. We'd have anything to help him, and we didn't even know him."

Liam watched a tear fall from Gabe's eye. Gabe exhaled, expelling all the air from his lungs as he wiped the tear away.

"I never even got to say goodbye to him," Liam's voice fell low and began to shake. "And he didn't even leave me anything to say goodbye. I just always thought that we'd make it out together. I remember meeting an aunt at my mom's funeral who told me and my brothers that we were going to beat this world, that everything we went through was just building us up to some great life someday, and I held onto that; that was my hope. Now I just wish I had just tried harder, just tried harder, and been more for him. He was always there for me, and when he needed me the most, I let him down. He was always there for me, and then he died all alone. All alone, without even knowing how much he meant to me. Maybe if he knew, this wouldn't have happened."

"No, Liam," Gabe interrupted. "You really have no idea how many times your love saved your brother's life. What happened to your brother was not your fault."

"How can it not be?" Liam cried. "I knew that he wasn't well. I stood by and watched as kids at school picked on him, watched my brother pick on him, watched as my own dad would hit him. I stood by and did nothing. How could this not be my fault?"

"This was not your fault because…" Gabe started, but Liam interrupted him.

"It should have been me," Liam said, almost like he was muttering to himself.

"Don't let your grief lie to you, Liam. It shouldn't have been you, and it shouldn't have been him. You both should still be here."

Liam wiped the tears that were freely flowing down his face and nodded. He knew that Gabe was right, and that it was not actually his fault. He himself would always tell others that their brains think so much faster than they speak, which is why it is important not to keep all these kinds of things bottled up in your own mind. Instead, it's good to talk them out.

"Gosh, guys," Brynn exhaled, looking like she was desperately trying to keep the floodgates from opening.

"What are your feelings about this, Brynn?" Gabe asked.

Brynn wiped her face on her sleeve, but she had not shed a tear. "I've never told anyone this, but some days I feel like I am fundamentally flawed. There are days that all I want to do is sleep like I can hardly get out of bed, but I just lie wide awake most nights, thinking about all the things that are wrong with me. Reliving every mistake I ever made and every conversation I ever had that I wish I could take back. I always wonder what's wrong with me, why I can't be like everyone else, why I have to work so hard just to do normal things that come so easily to everyone. So many times, I'd make plans to get together with someone on the weekend because I'd think that I could handle it until the day got closer, and my anxiety took over, and I'd cancel all my plans. I've lost all my friends because of it. I've thought about ending my life so many times in this last year, but I disguise how I'm feeling with a smile. When others talk about the future, I feel nothing, like I don't see a future for myself at all. It wasn't until I met Liam and heard about his mission that I felt any sort of purpose for myself, like I could be of any use to anyone."

"Don't either of you ever underestimate the impact that would be felt by your absence," Gabe said, his eyes and voice matching in sincerity. "You both have so much left to give this world. Your brother left this world far too soon, and that's an unbelievable tragedy. I'm so sorry you're hurting, but I don't think he'd want you to blame yourself."

"I know that he wouldn't," Liam agreed, breathing heavily through his mouth, his nose too stuffy from crying to let any air in.

"Now," Gabe said with a smile, "let's get to that hill before we lose the light."

The three walked quietly for a while, with a lightheartedness in the air. Although Liam still felt a deep sadness over the loss of his brother, he felt light as a feather as the weight of guilt had been lifted off of him. He looped Gabe's words on repeat in his mind so he had something to tell himself if ever the lance of guilt were to take a stab at him again.

"Can I ask you something else, Gabe?" Liam asked. As Gabe nodded to him so, Liam continued. "Were you always like this? I mean, were you always homeless, or did you become homeless?"

Liam noticed that Gabe always took a long pause before he answered any question. "No, I wasn't always like this," he finally answered, taking a deep breath as he smiled to himself, deep in memory. "You wouldn't think to look at me now, but I used to be someone that others looked up to and respected. I had a home, a job, a car. I even had a white picket fence, and everything I held dear was inside of it. I guess things changed for me after I left the military. I tried to pick up where I left off, but I didn't know how hard it would be to do that."

"I'm sorry," Liam said, seeing how talking about it had changed Gabe's face, which no longer looked aged by time but by pain.

"No need to be sorry, Liam. We all have a story, and I don't mind sharing mine." Gabe stopped in the middle of the road, lifting his left pant leg, exposing a large, thick scar that ran down the entire back of his leg. "I was injured in the line of duty, and when I was sent home, I wasn't able to get a job on account of my injury." Gabe pulled his pant leg down and continued, "Slowly, things just started slipping through my fingers. One by one, almost day by day, I lost everything. So no, I wasn't always this way." Gabe paused again in reflection. "I can't really say I lost everything. I was choosing to drink over everything; my choices destroyed everything."

"Really? You?" Liam asked. "Now that I've gotten to know you, I'd never think that you ever had a problem with drinking."

"Well, Liam, the truth is, I never had a problem with drinking. In my mind, I was having a great time. It was sobriety that I struggled with. You can take the veteran out of the war, but you can't take the war out of the veteran. But by the time I realized how much I'd thrown away, my drinking had already severed every root my life had. I don't blame those who left me behind," Gabe smiled and glanced out the side of his eye at Liam, trying to reassure him that despite how heavy the question was, he was still happy to answer it. "I've been very blessed in my life. I've met great people along the way, and I'm thankful for that."

"So, do you think that anyone can stop drinking?" Liam asked.

"I do," Gabe replied, "but it's something that they have to choose for themselves. I'm ashamed to say that no amount of begging and pleading from anyone can make that choice for them. I know it didn't for me."

Liam thought about his own father, wondering if this could ever be a choice that he would make.

"How do you do it?" Liam asked. "How do you carry on with your life when you've lost everything? How do you pick up every day and go on?"

"It isn't always easy. I can tell you that much for sure. Life has definitely thrown me some curve balls—some fast ones! But I just take it step by step, day by day. Each and every day I spend my time trying to do the right thing, trying to see where I can be of good use, whatever that looks like day in and day out. I know that living my life with purpose and doing it on purpose is all that matters."

"But how do you know what the right thing to do is? How will I know where the truth lies in my own life?" Liam asked, his voice almost shaking.

"That's just it, Liam," Gabe smiled. "The truth never lies. That's how you know what the right thing to do is. Life may never seem black and white, but what's right and wrong is."

"Well, I'll tell you what, I don't need any more hard times to develop my character," Brynn announced. "My character is developed enough, thank you!"

Liam laughed, and did not ask any more questions, but his mind circled around the conversation. Gabe really was as wise as Brynn said, and Liam put his mind to work, trying to think of more questions to ask him, but nothing came to mind.

The rest of the walk was spent in light-hearted conversation. Brynn mostly asked Gabe random questions, trying to keep the conversation light-hearted and not too deep. They all shared some good laughs as they walked down the long, winding road until the sun began descending into the west, and the three knew it would be dark within a couple of hours.

"We don't have too much further to go now," Brynn said, "and thank goodness for that." Holding her fingers up to the sun and counting how many fingers were between the sun and the ground, she said, "We're about to lose the light!"

"I have a question for you now, Brynn," Liam said.

Brynn eyed over Liam skeptically before nodding her head towards him.

"Why is it that your classmates call you Barley? I mean, other than the clever play on your name."

"Ugh," Brynn groaned in reply. "Can we not? I was really hoping that you would have forgotten about this by now."

The expression on Liam's face said all Brynn needed to know that he was not going to give up that easily.

"Okay, so basically," Brynn stalled, "when I was in the fourth grade, I was eating soup, and in front of everyone,

I dropped it onto the floor, and just because of the way that it fell, it shot up and covered everything from the roof to me, to the tables. It was barley soup.”

Liam laughed, even though he had told himself that no matter what she had told him, he would not. Brynn glared at him, sparks flying through her eyes like a knife being sharpened on a stone.

“I'm sorry, Brynn,” Liam laughed. “It's kind of funny!”

“Okay, Chicken Legs,” Brynn spat, “I don't even need to ask why you were given that nickname!”

Liam did not take the shot personally. After all, he just laughed at Brynn's nickname. Liam just smiled at her, and she returned a toothful grin back.

“Just around this last corner is Graffiti Hill!” Brynn announced.

Liam felt his heart speed up in anticipation, and he had not noticed he had started walking twice as fast as he had been.

Finally, Liam stood in front of it, Graffiti Hill, which was more of a small cliff on a pull-out on the side of the road than it was a hill, rising well above the surrounding landscape, seeming to rise up out of nowhere. The entire surface of the rocky cliff was covered with graffiti. Some were faded and peeling, worn and chipped. Others were bright and bold, their colours still vivid. Layers upon layers of aging paint, tags, and murals, all evident of the countless artists that had come to leave their mark.

"It's incredible!" Liam whispered. He was not sure why he whispered it. There was something eerie about the silence of this place.

On the ground below the cliff was a firepit made of large rocks built into a circle, and the chard wood and layer of fresh ash was evidence that kids did still come up to the hill often. Around the firepit were logs arranged as seats, and that is where Gabe sat down while Liam and Brynn walked around the bottom of the hill, looking for anything that looked familiar to the signature or train art on Liam's camera. Liam took a step closer, running his finger against the worn-down paint. A thick dust layer stuck to his finger, and he ran it across.

Nothing looked familiar. Looking at all the art, none of them found anything that looked like the signature in the picture on his camera. Finally, after a reasonable search, Liam admitted defeat and sat down beside Gabe, his face looking heavy with disappointment.

"I'm really sorry that this was a dead end, Liam," Brynn said, sitting next to him, who looked depleted as he sunk his head into his hands.

"It's all good," Liam replied. "We all knew that it was a long shot coming out here." Liam placed his backpack beside him, and after returning the camera to the front pocket, he zipped it closed again.

The three agreed to rest before heading out on their long walk back to town. October nights rolled in fast, and as the sun sank beneath a backdrop of silhouette trees and into the shadows of faraway hills, it left behind a palette of fiery red and orange sky. But with the sun went its warmth, and a chill returned, filling the air with a crisp sharpness again. In the wake of the new darkness, the night's first stars spread across the sky, and the pale moon hung so brightly above that it cast strange shadows all around them. Everything in the night seemed still, except for the grass in the fields that danced in the light breeze.

Liam lifted his head up, looking back at the hill and casting shadows with his flashlight on the cliff as he stared at the art on the jagged rocks. He was entirely out of clues, leads, and ideas. Liam closed his eyes for a moment until a shrilling sound had him lifted to his feet quickly. He shone his flashlight around, and in the far distance, he heard it again; it was howling.

"Don't worry, Liam. Those are just some coyotes, and they sound far off," Brynn said encouragingly, walking over and standing beside him. "Besides, they sound like they're coming from further up from the road, not the direction we'll be heading back to town."

Liam smiled as he sat back down, trying to choke back his disappointment about his mission and his nerves about the wild animals. Brynn sat back down next to him, smiling back.

"We should start heading back pretty soon," Gabe said, standing over them.

Liam nodded his head but said nothing. he stood up again, taking one last look over the paint-layered cliff before looking back towards town. The road back seemed longer in the dark, and ahead of them, in the far distance, they could see the overhead glow of the city lights. The highway across the fields that ran alongside the dirt road was still busy with the headlights of passing cars, but that felt like a long way away now as Liam looked up the long stretch of road back to town.

"Listen, kid," Gabe leaned towards Liam. "Just because the plan changes doesn't mean the goal has. Sometimes, things don't work out, and you may find your goal and your mission aren't even the same thing."

Liam smiled at Gabe graciously but was unsure if he fully understood what he meant. "I just feel bad. I wasted your entire day on this wild goose chase, and now I'm not any closer to getting this letter to them, either."

"I think we all took a lot from our adventure today," Gabe smiled softly and nodded.

"I'll tell you what," Brynn said, brushing a fine layer of dust off her pants. "I'm going to need a shower after this long day on the road!"

Liam smiled again, smacking his flashlight, which was now flashing off and on. "The batteries must be running out," he said, giving it another smack against his leg, and again, it lit up. "Hopefully, it'll last the walk back."

Liam jumped and the flashlight was now shaking in his hand as another howl broke the silence of the night air. This one seemed closer than the last but was still some distance away. Maybe it was a trick of the night or the noise echoing off the fields and hills around them, but the first howl was quickly followed by a second one, but closer to where the three were now standing. Liam turned around quickly, flashing his light along the open fields around them. Clouds drifted across the sky, hiding the moon and leaving the landscape shadowless, and nothing beyond Liam's dimming flashlight was visible. Reflecting in the light, they could see that scattering in the surrounding fields were pale, white eyes, beaming back at them in the light and crawling closer and closer, the dead grass bowing under their steps and shriveling beneath them. Liam turned in circles, but his dimming light was not enough to know the actual numbers that surrounded them. Everywhere he turned his light were more eyes, and they were completely surrounded.

"They're wolves!" Brynn shrieked, rushing over to the road where Liam was standing, feeling some sense of protection in the light of the flashlight.

"No, I think they're coyotes!" Liam cried back, turning around quickly and flashing his light again in every direction, smacking it again as it had shut off again. Between their own heavy breaths and hearts beating like drums, the three could hear the crumpling of leaves under footsteps that were getting closer and closer to the road where they were standing in the middle of.

"No, those are way too big just to be coyotes!" Brynn shouted.

"Be very quiet," said Gabe, walking towards Liam and Brynn. He tried to keep his voice steady and calm, but Liam could hear the shake of fear as he spoke.

Liam's light flashed on again, and he kept it fixed on the open fields, his eyes burning from his fierce concentration. The more he shined it around, the more eyes became visible, and the howling became louder and louder as it got closer until they felt as though the sound was almost right on top of them, closing in and surrounding them. The light trembled in Liam's hand as he thought about trying to run to one of the houses they had passed on their walk there. But they were surrounded, and Liam knew the three could not outrun them, especially in the dark night.

"What do we do?" Brynn whispered, trying to inch closer into the circle they were now standing in.

Her question went unanswered.

Liam ground his chattering teeth, trying to hide the sound of fear, and he saturated his hand as he pulled it across his sweating forehead, again smacking his flashlight in a panic against his leg. The light flashed back on, and Liam pointed it as steady as he could again at the field. Whatever was in the fields, either wolves or coyotes, they were close enough now that the snarls and snapping of their teeth could be heard. Brynn, Liam, and Gabe stepped closer together, with Liam and his failing flashlight in the middle.

"We should yell. If we sound loud enough, they should run off," Brynn suggested, remembering reading that somewhere. The three began yelling as loudly as they could, shouting and screaming and grunting and groaning, but the shadows flashed across the flashlight's light, and the pale eyes continued to get closer and closer.

The flashlight went out again, and Liam frantically hit it against his leg repeatedly, but it did not come back on. Then, suddenly, the three found themselves surrounded by light. Not just onto the field, but it completely engulfed them in the middle of the road and illuminated everything around them. At once, the three turned around, and from behind them, coming up the dirt road, were headlights approaching fast. The beams of eyes scattered from the light into the darkness as the car got closer. The sound of the howls became distant, and the eyes faded into the shadows of the field until they were no longer visible, and the sounds pushed further into the distant trees of the forest that lined the farthest fields.

"The car scared them off!" Liam said, taking a deep breath of relief, trying to steady his shaking heart and legs.

"Let's get off the road before that car reaches us, too," Brynn said. "I doubt they've seen us yet, but I've never been one to trust meeting a car on a back dirt road in the dead of night!"

Gabe and Liam followed Brynn as she ran down into the ditch and back up the side of the field, where they knew they would be out of sight from the vehicle still quickly approaching. They crawled under the barbed wire fence that separated the field from the road and hid behind a bale of hay that sat on the edge of the field. The car sped by them and stopped in a cloud of dust, red from the brake lights, in the pull-out off the road under Graffiti Hill.

"Phew, not a cop car!" Brynn said, brushing her hands together.

The three stayed hidden as they watched as two teenage boys, who looked like they could be the same age as Liam and Brynn, jumped out of the car. In the light of the headlights, and with the sound of the music blasting from the stereo, the two boys started a fire in the rock pit. The thick smoke rose from the fire pit, twisting above the dancing orange flames as the boys placed more wood on top. They could hear the boys laughing around the crackling of the open fire and cracking the tops off their beers.

"Let's get out of here, kids," Gabe said calmly, "if we just walk up the field a ways, we should keep out of their sights, and once we turn the corner, we should be able to get back onto the road."

"We don't have a working flashlight," Liam said, smacking it against his hand one more time for good measure.

"You got any batteries in your backpack?" Brynn asked.

"My backpack!" Liam shouted. "I left it beside the fire pit!"

Chapter 17

~Courage Under Fire~

The moonlight shifted through the high grass as it swayed in the gentle wind, almost in rhythm with the music that hummed in the distance from the firepit. Liam felt a flood of nerves wash over him. He did not want to interact with these boys, but he also knew he had no choice and could not walk back to town without his backpack and letter.

"I bet we could sneak down there and grab your bag completely unnoticed," Brynn said excitedly, as if it were just some sort of game to her.

"You kids go on, I'll wait here for you," Gabe suggested. "I'm not as quiet as you kids can be. Shout out if you need me. I'll be right here."

Liam and Brynn left Gabe in the field and walked down the ditch, hidden in the trench, following the glow of the fire.

"It looks close enough to the ditch that we could probably sneak over there and grab it without being seen," Brynn whispered to Liam once they were close enough to see the backpack sitting by the logs at the fire. "I don't think they've seen your bag. But we'll have to be pretty stealthy. I think if you and I sneak up along the backside of the car we could then sneak around and grab your bag, but we'll have to be silent if we're going to do this without them noticing."

Liam and Brynn went through the dead grass and knotted roots along the ditch as quietly as possible, cutting their hands and stubbing their knees as they crawled through. Liam looked back and saw Gabe's shadow kneeling against the haybale in the field. Luckily, all the noise from the loud music from the car stereo mixed with the crackling of the fire silenced the little noise that Brynn and Liam made. Liam looked ahead, trying to find a clear path that would make the least amount of noise and stay out of the two boys' sight.

"Well, isn't this an amper-upper!" Brynn laughed in a loud whisper. Liam just shook his head at her. He was genuinely afraid, and the fact that she was not made him somewhat uncomfortable.

The fire had grown bigger and swallowed all the wood, and was now being filled again by one of the boys. The large flame provided some more light, and now Brynn and Liam could see the two boys' faces.

"Do you recognize either of them?" Liam asked in a low, cautious tone once they were close enough to see them more clearly.

Brynn looked over their faces in the light of the fire, "The taller one is definitely Colin McClain. He's in a grade ahead of us. I don't know the other one's name, but I recognize him. I don't know them well, but I've heard horror stories from people who do. They're as nasty as they come. Whatever you do, don't get caught. Let's get your bag and get the heck outta here."

Liam agreed, and they made their way down the ditch and mostly back up to the road until they were as close as they could go without being seen. Colin and his friend were sitting along the two far logs with their back to the road, filling the fire with more logs from the back of their car, building the fire up, and unfortunately, the light from it as well, meaning there was less darkness for Brynn and Liam to hide in. Although they were seated on the logs farthest away from the backpack and had not yet noticed it, they were facing where it lay on the ground.

"We need to figure out a way to get their attention away so we can quickly grab the bag and go!" Brynn said in a hushed whisper, her face flickering in the light of the fire. "I have an idea." Her eyes brightened, and she shot a mischievous smile at Liam. "I'm going to distract them. When they're not looking, grab the bag."

"What are you going to do?" Liam asked, but Brynn was gone, disappearing into the shadows of the night without answering him.

Liam cowered low to the ground, feeling uncomfortable that Brynn had made a plan and had not shared it with him. Liam lay flat on his stomach, ensuring he was still able to see the boys from where he was lying. Liam lay for quite a while, watching the teenagers while tracing Brynn's movements as she crawled like a snake through the grass. He only caught a glimpse sometimes when the top of the grass moved in the firelight. Then Liam caught Brynn in the corner of his eye, watching as she crawled behind where the car was parked. Liam waited for any sign of what Brynn had planned. The two teenagers were still facing Liam's backpack, and he could not grab it unseen. Then, as Liam watched, he could see tiny rocks spatter and hit the road, and he assumed this was Brynn's attempt at distracting the teenage boys and getting their attention away from his direction. Again, the road was spattered with rocks, but the music from the car and the fire crackling were too loud for them to even notice Brynn throwing the stones into the road. Liam watched as Brynn tried again, but they still heard nothing. Liam was unsure if Brynn had changed her tactic or if she did it by mistake, but next, Liam heard many of the rocks hitting the car. Both boys stood up and slowly walked towards their car, looking more confused than angry.

While their backs were to him, Liam scurried up through the grass onto his feet and ran to the open space by the fire pit to his backpack, keeping his eye on the boys who were no longer looking at the car and were now looking over the ridge of the other side of the road, right where Brynn had been hiding. Just as Liam was about to grab his bag, both boys must have heard him and were now dashing towards him. Liam tried to run into the cloak of darkness, but just as he turned to run, he felt a strong hand on his shoulder, grabbing him and pulling him to the ground.

Liam fell backward onto the ground, his hands filling with gravel and the dust from the road filled his nose and mouth. Liam turned around, lying on his back with the two older boys standing over him. The boy, whom Brynn pointed out to be Colin, grabbed him, pulled him up to his feet, grabbed his backpack out of his hand, and handed it to his friend.

Now that Liam could look closer, the two boys were much taller than him. They reminded him of his father as they smacked him around with the smell of beer and smoke on their breath, and there was something about the reflection of the fire that danced in their eyes that only emanated anger in them as they spat disgusting words and curses at him.

"What's a kid like you doing all the way out here by yourself?" Colin said, looking down at Liam, his hands balled into a fist. He did not wait for Liam to answer before he continued. "Was that you throwing rocks at our car?" He dug his thumb deep into Liam's shoulder.

"Please, I really don't want any trouble," Liam said, trying to grab his backpack. "I just forgot my bag here and came back to grab it."

"Well, you found trouble!" Colin promised, laughing at the other boy beside him.

"Please, just give me my bag, and I'll leave." Liam pleaded.

"This?" Colin's friend asked, holding Liam's backpack beside his face. "This is our backpack now. Besides, why do you want to leave so quick? Don't you want to stay and have some fun with us?"

Liam did not answer, trying to remember to breathe amid his fear.

"What's in here that's so important? Let's just sit down together and see." Each of them grabbed Liam by the arms, dragging him over to the log seats, then pulling him down by his shoulders, and there he sat between them.

"Now I know what you must be thinking," Colin said. "You must be thinking that you could just grab your bag and run, but I really hope you're not that stupid. We have a car, and driving down these back fields is just sport around here. There's two of us and one of you."

Just as Colin had finished speaking and almost on cue, Brynn jumped out from the darkness into the light of the fire.

"Hey, you psychological toxic waste bombs! Leave him alone!" She shouted, charging at them.

Brynn's scared them enough that they both jumped to their feet. While the two boys were distracted, Liam grabbed his backpack and ran. Liam ran as fast as he could, his heart accelerating more and more as he ran up the hill to the field. But when Liam looked behind him, he realized Brynn was not running behind him. He looked around, hoping she had found a different way up to the field. He took a few steps back to the fire, and then, without hesitation, he began to run back to see if he could see her. As he came running into the opening and light of the fire, Liam could see a third silhouette sitting down on one of the logs by the fire, the two boys standing over her.

"Leave her alone!" Liam wailed, running until he was standing right in front of them.

Colin walked over to Liam and, without even muttering a word, punched him in the stomach, and he fell to the ground. Colin grabbed Liam's backpack off his shoulder as he fell. As Colin walked away, the other grabbed Liam by his hair and lifted him into a kneel. "You should have just run," he said, jolting Liam's head back with a fistful of hair until his chin was pointing to the night sky. Across from him, standing in the light of the fire, was Colin, holding a knife in his hand, testing its sharpness in minor scrapes across his thumb.

"Why are you doing this?" Brynn cried out.

Colin, while still holding the knife, walked next to her and bent down to her ear, saying loud enough for Liam to hear over the cracking of the fire, "Because we can!" and then let out a laugh that curdled Liam's blood.

The other still stood with Liam, holding a fist full of his hair. Colin walked over and bent down to Liam, teasing Liam's neck with the blade. Colin stood up, nodding his head to his friend, indicating him to lift Liam to his feet. Suddenly, Liam heard a loud shout, and without a chance for anyone to react, Brynn jumped from behind onto Colin's back. Her arms tightly grasped around his neck as she tried to swing him down onto the ground. They struggled, and Liam tried to break free of the hold the second had on him so that he could go and help Brynn. As Liam fought, his ribs felt like they splintered as he got a kick into his side from Colin's friend. Liam held his ribs, struggling to catch his breath after all the wind had been knocked from his lungs. Liam looked up to Brynn, and just as he did, Brynn was thrown off his back and fell down hard, hitting her head on the ground.

"Brynn!" Liam's eyes widened, as fear gave way to panic. But she did not answer as she lay motionless on the ground.

All the blood drained from Liam's face as Colin stood back on his feet, grabbing the knife off the ground where it had fallen and after dusting himself off, began walking towards Brynn, almost growling in anger. Liam took in as big of a breath as he could and pulled his head down as far as he could manage, and with all his strength, and through the pain of many of his hairs being torn out from their roots, he smashed the back of his head up into the chin of his own capturer. Colin's friend fell to the ground, covering his mouth and groaning in pain. Liam charged at Colin, and for the first time in his life, he did not question himself about the danger or weigh out his options. Although he had no idea where the courage came from, he charged at full speed.

All he knew at the moment was that he could not stand to watch what was about to happen to Brynn, especially since he was all too aware that everything that had already happened to her was his fault. He knocked Colin to the ground, the knife falling only a few feet away. Liam pushed off the ground onto his hands and feet, crawling as fast as he could to reach it before the other could. Liam could hear the loud footsteps of the second boy as he dragged his feet across the dirt as he ran behind him. He felt a smash to the back of his head as Colin's friend kicked him. Liam fell onto his face, breathing in the dirt, unable to lift himself up again. He watched Brynn stand up, cupping her forehead in her hand.

Liam lifted his head as much as he could. The night sky was suddenly lit up in blue and red flashes as he watched Colin and his friend trip over each other in a panic. The two boys got to their car and drove away.

"Liam," Brynn crawled over, "Liam! The cops are here. we have to go!" Liam tried to stand, but the pounding in the back of his head sent the world spinning around him.

"I'll be right back, Liam. I'm going to get Gabe. Don't go anywhere. I'll be right back." The surrounding light faded, and the commotion sounded farther away until all that he could hear was his pulse pounding in his ears. Liam watched as everything around him slipped away into darkness.

Chapter 18

~ Rekindling Kinship ~

Liam was dead. Or at least that is what he thought, as he felt a strange tinge in his veins and the mind-numbing ache in his head as he tried to lift himself off the ground. He opened his eyes to see someone standing over him, calling him back to himself. "Jacob?" Liam called out, *"I must be dead,"* he thought to himself as he failed to lift himself off of the ground. But as his double vision came into focus on the face above him, he realized, "Drew?" he asked, sounding more surprised to see him than if it really was Jacob standing there. Drew pulled Liam to his feet, holding him up until he found his balance. "What are you doing here?"

Drew did not have a chance to answer before Gabe and Brynn came running up from behind him. Brynn rushed at Drew and began punching him in the back. "Get off him, you big bully!" She shouted, landing a few more punches.

Drew turned around, holding his arm against the top of Brynn's head as she swung punches and kicked her legs out at him, none of them even reaching him.

"Stop Brynn!" Liam shouted. "He's my brother!"

"Your brother?" Brynn said as she backed away. She looked over at Drew, her face wrinkled. "Well, this is awkward."

"How did you find me?" Liam asked in disbelief. He thought about everything that had happened over the last few days. Could Drew really have followed him everywhere they had gone without him noticing?

"You really think I was going to let you come all this way alone?" Drew asked. "I've been watching you, just waiting for you to get in some sort of trouble. A few times, I almost blew my cover, but thank goodness you were too distracted by everything else to notice. I told you that police light was going to come in handy someday!”

“Well, why did you have to leave and come find me? Did reporting me missing not get me home fast enough for you?”

Drew looked at Liam, his head slightly tilted to the right, and his eyes narrowed as he tried to make sense of what Liam had said. “I never reported you missing Liam.”

“Sure, you didn’t. Who did then? Dad?” Liam scoffed.

“I left the same night you did. I was even parked outside the school when you first got there. But I figured I’d wait for you to get into real trouble and let you have your fun for a bit. You should be thanking me for chasing off those kids for you before they could cause any real dam…”

“The letter!” Liam interrupted, looking around the fire pit, now just coals and embers dimming away, “My backpack!”

“It’s gone,” Brynn reluctantly told him. “They took it!”

"It's gone? My backpack, the letter, it's all gone?"

"When they saw the police light, or I guess, your brother's lights, they grabbed your backpack and took off in their car," Brynn said. "They can't have gotten too far, though. Let's jump in the car and catch them!"

"No, Brynn," Liam fell, recovering himself, and sat on the ground, holding his pounding head in his hands. He sat down, his body empty of all its energy. "You could have gotten seriously hurt tonight, and for what?" Liam asked. "For me to chase some ghost I'll likely never find. I pretend that I'm doing this for Jacob, but I'm doing this for me. So that I don't feel like I'm just a failure who let my brother down."

Drew sat beside Liam, putting his hand over his shoulder. "I'm sorry this happened, Liam. But now it's time to go home. You did your best, and now it's time to move on."

"So, you got what you wanted." Liam stood up, pushing Drew's hand from his shoulder. "So now you get to say that you told me so?"

"Liam, this isn't about me saying I told you so. It's about me keeping you safe."

"Keeping me safe? How can you even say that? You've never cared about keeping me safe. Like you never cared about keeping Jacob safe," Liam snapped back at Drew as he had never before, with little thought about how his words might hurt him. "Look where all your 'I told you so' got him!" As soon as those words left Liam's lips, he felt the instant sting of regret. He knew Jacob's death was no more Drew's fault than it was his own, and he knew that he had no right to hit with such a low blow just to get his point across about how he was feeling. Liam looked at Gabe and could see either sympathy or disappointment across his face, but he could not be sure of which.

A silence fell around them. No one said another word for too long for Liam's liking, leaving his words to echo through the night, magnified by the stillness in the air as the adrenaline from the evening's events began to wear off. Drew stood up and stepped back. The weight of Liam's words seemed to hit him like a door in the face. Drew stomped back towards his car, kicking the dirt as he walked. He opened the car door, and as he went to get in, he quickly changed his mind, slamming the door closed again, and he began storming back to Liam. With anger in his voice, he yelled at Liam,

"Don't you think I feel guilty about what happened? Don't you realize that I do blame myself?" The sharpness in Drew's voice suddenly dissipated, replaced with the sound of dull pain. "All I was trying to do was make you guys stronger, because if you weren't strong, then the world would break you! That's all I was trying to do with Jacob." Drew was crying now, all at once, like he had been holding every tear he ever had in, and they were now coming out all at once.

"Drew-I," Liam's voice broke. Drew had always told him that showing his feelings was weakness, and that someone was always waiting to use his weakness against him. Now, as Drew cried so heavily in front of him, Liam did not know what to do.

Drew continued through his tears. "I never got the chance to tell him how much I cared. When I would step in front of Dad, that was me standing up for him, trying to keep him from being hit again in the only way I knew how. Sometimes, when it sounded like I agreed with Dad, it was to make him not get more angry and get Jacob more hurt. I was trying to smarten him up so he wouldn't get into those situations. But now he's gone, and I'll never get the chance to make it right with him or the chance to tell him that I thought the world of him, that I was proud of him in so many ways!" Drew wiped the tears from his face. Still, new ones fell as soon as he had wiped them. "But now, I can't lose you too. You are all I have left in this world, and I have to protect you!"

"I'm sorry," Liam said, his salted tears clinging to his face. He hugged Drew as tight as his tired body could, and for the first time in his life, he felt he could comfort him. Drew fell deeply into the hug and sat in Liam's arms as he continued to cry. Liam lifted his head. "I didn't realize all of that," Liam said.

The two brothers sat together, Liam's arm around Drew as he cried into his forearm. Drew lifted his head and looked at Liam, wiping another tear off his chin as he tried to compose himself. "I am sorry, Liam."

"I know," Liam said with a comforting smile. "I'm sorry too."

No more words were spoken for a few minutes. The two just sat together and cried, which was quite overdue.

"Well, now that's all out of the way. Can we go and get that letter back?" Brynn asked. She felt somewhat awkward about all the emotions being thrown around.

"What do you mean?" Liam asked. "My backpack is gone. Besides, it's too dangerous."

"I've roughed up a few kids in my day," Drew laughed. "These kids don't scare me!"

"And you forgot what an amazing super detective I am," Brynn laughed, "Okay, so I told you I recognized the one kid, Colin. Well, I also know exactly where he lives."

Liam had never been so excited to hop into the back seat of Ol' Rusty as he was that night. He even found comfort in the musky smell and the way that it hummed loudly down the open road.

Liam watched as the fields and farmhouses quickly passed by from the backseat car window. All were quiet on the drive, and the radio quietly flickered in and out with static until Drew finally decided to shut it off. Then the only sound was from the car as it shook down the bumpy road. Liam looked across to Brynn. Her head was slouched against the window, and her eyes were closed. Gabe, too, had fallen asleep in the passenger seat. Liam could hear him snoring. Liam wanted to sleep, but as he could see the lights from town fast approaching, he figured there was no point in trying. Liam looked into the rear-view mirror, where he could see in the dim light from the headlights that Drew was already looking at him.

"Thanks for doing this, Drew." Liam smiled and looked back out the window.

As they reached the light of the edge of town, Liam nudged Brynn awake. She sat up, quickly rubbing the sleep out of her eyes. "Sorry," she said, "I must have dozed off."

"It's all good," Liam said. "We're almost to town."

Brynn looked outside the window and instructed Drew on each turn and road to get to Colin's house.

"That one there," Brynn said, pointing her finger to the left side of the road to a white house.

"There's no car in the driveway," Liam said, sitting back in his seat.

"What do you want to do now?" Drew asked. "Just wait for him to come back?"

"Let's just drive around," Brynn suggested, "there isn't much open this time of night. With some luck, we might just see them driving around."

By now, it was late into the night, and most of the houses along the streets were dark, with only a few porch lights on. The four drove to the intersection at the end of the road, and with no specific destination in mind, they continued to drive down the residential area. Liam wondered why Ol' Rusty sounded louder than usual as it clunked down the quiet streets.

"Do you guys hear that?" Liam asked as they rounded down another block.

"Sounds like thumping?" Brynn answered.

Drew turned the heat off, which was humming in the front seat, to have a better listen. "Well, what can I say," Drew said, "it's an old car."

"No, it's not the car, shhhh," Brynn hushed. "Listen."

Everyone in the car sat silent. As they continued driving, they could all hear a constant beat that grew louder and louder.

"It's coming from the yellow house," Drew said as they got closer to the sound and the music got louder.

As they parked outside the yellow house, the music thumped so hard that the windows in Ol' Rusty raddled to the beat. Cars lined the street and filled the driveway, and scattered across the lawn were a bunch of people dancing and shouting in the yard. As they got close enough to see through the windows, there were even more people, so many that to Liam, it looked like the house must be about to bust open.

"It looks like a house party," Drew said, "a pretty rowdy one too."

"Look!" Brynn shouted. "That's Colin's car!"

"That's definitely the same car they took out to Graffiti Hill! That's it!" Liam agreed.

Chapter 19

~ Party Pursuit ~

"Well, with any luck, the backpack will be in it," Gabe said. "Pull in behind it, and I'll go look in it."

Drew parked behind the car, and Gabe crept along the side of it, looking around to make sure no one would see him. He then jumped inside. Drew, Brynn, and Liam waited inside Drew's car, keeping watch so that they could alert Gabe if anyone was coming.

"It's not in there," Gabe said as he jumped back into the car's front seat.

"Well, now what?" Brynn asked. "Should we go inside and see if we can find it?"

"That's one idea," Drew said. "There are enough people inside that we could probably blend right in."

"Not me," Gabe said. "I'll wait here. I think it would be a lot harder for the three of you to blend in with an old man with you kids." Gabe leaned the passenger seat back a bit, cupping the back of his head on his intertwined fingers, and closed his eyes.

With that, Brynn, Liam, and Drew walked in the front door and did what they could to blend in. Drew pulled open the front door, and the sounds of shouting and laughter beneath the music volume hit the three like a wave and ran through them like a heartbeat. The smell of alcohol, sweat, and cheap perfume made their eyes water, and the packed living room and kitchen that they could see from the front door made them feel claustrophobic before they even walked inside.

"There's nothing more fun than being sober at a house party," Drew shouted over the noise as the three walked into the house, closing the door behind them. No one looked over or even noticed them walk inside. Brynn looked to the corner of the living room, where she recognized a small group of kids huddled together in the corner of the room, sipping out of their red plastic cups.

"There's Mark and some other kids from school," Brynn said, nodding her head in their direction. Mark turned away, pretending not to notice them at all and laughing to his group of friends. "We should split up," Brynn suggested. "We can cover more ground that way. The faster we can get outta here, the better."

The brothers reluctantly agreed, and they split up. Liam expected Brynn to walk over and talk to Mark and the other kids from her class, but instead, he watched as she pushed past the wall of people and walked up the stairs opposite the kitchen.

"Meet back here soon," Drew said to Liam before walking through a thick haze of smoke onto the back porch.

Liam tried to blend in with the crowd and walked into the living room and over to where Mark was standing.

"Hey, Mark!" Liam said with a wave in his direction.

"Hey! This is the kid I was telling you about!" Mark slurred, shouting to his friend and nudging him by the shoulder. "Did you finally get some common sense and ditch Barley?"

Everyone in the group laughed, but not Liam. He stood without an expression.

"What do you mean?" Liam asked, breaking up the group's laughter.

"You're funny," a girl in the group said, sending them all laughing again. Liam stood for a moment longer but finally decided to walk away, realizing that the group was not going to be much help to him.

Just as Liam was about to walk away, he turned back to the group. "You know what? You guys can make fun of Brynn in any way you like. But you don't even know her. She's the most honest, true friend anyone could ever have. I am so happy to know her!"

The group said nothing, speechlessly standing before Liam as he turned back around and walked away. From there, Liam walked from the living room to the kitchen. In just that short walk across the two rooms, he saw one girl crying uncontrollably to a friend, one girl dancing on the coffee table while her friends tried to pull her down, one guy getting punched in the face, and someone back in the living room broke a vase. It felt like chaos all around him.

Liam looked out the kitchen window that overlooked the back porch. He could see Drew talking to someone outside. Liam decided to try to find his backpack by going through the house from room to room, starting in the kitchen and working his way to the back of the house. Maybe it had been placed down when Colin and his friend arrived at the party and was, hopefully, not being carried around with them.

Liam started his search in the kitchen. He looked over the table and the counters. Finding nothing, he then walked into the hallway.

"What are you doing?" a voice shouted from behind him when he had opened a closet door. He quickly came behind Liam and slammed the door closed.

"I'm, I," Liam searched for an acceptable answer to why he was snooping through closets. "I'm just looking for the bathroom."

"Down the hallway, last door on the left," he said. He then stood and watched as Liam walked down the hallway to the bathroom and returned to the kitchen. Liam tried the bathroom door, but it was locked. He walked to the back porch, where Drew was still standing. He found him talking to a few people. One was the guy who had just caught him going through the kitchen closet.

"Well, hopefully, Drew can keep him distracted enough that he won't bother me anymore," Liam thought.

Drew, laughing away on the deck with his new friends, did not notice Liam as he walked outside. Liam pulled on Drew's sweater, pulling him aside. "I've looked over most of downstairs. I'm going to check with Brynn to see if she's found anything upstairs." Drew waved him away and went back to his new friends.

Liam walked back inside and stood at the bottom of the stairs, looking around to make sure no one was watching, and then he crept up, tip-towing slowly and stepping over a girl who had passed out about three steps up, slumped against the wall. Liam found an eery silence upstairs, but beneath his feet, Liam could hear the music beating through the floor and heard the muffled laughs and shouting of partygoers downstairs. Liam stood for a moment at the top of the stairs. He found himself in a long hallway lined with doors, all closed. At the end of the hallway was a desk against the wall, and on the desk was a lamp that was lit. That was the only light, leaving the hallway dim and hard for Liam to see. On the wall to Liam's right were two sets of class photos, walking through the school years.

"That's Colin's friend," Liam whispered to himself, recognizing the kid aging through the photographs from a kindergartener with missing front teeth to the tall, angry bully he had experienced earlier in the night. Liam looked over the next set of pictures, recognizing them, too. "Oh, and that guy downstairs must be his brother," Liam said to himself again. "That explains why he was so worried about the closet. Hopefully Drew can get some information from him."

Liam had decided to check each room for Brynn, making sure no one else was upstairs before he started looking through them for his backpack. Liam stepped one doorway at a time down the hallway, listening at each before opening them and then closing them again. Liam had made his way by the first and second doors, but as Liam listened at the third, he could hear someone speaking on the other side but could not make out what was being said. Liam pushed his ear against the door, using his hands to cup around his ear.

"Stop it!" a voice from behind the door shouted, and Liam recognized it.

"Brynn!" Liam shouted as he pushed through the door. Colin sat on a bed, his friend on a chair beside the bed, and on the floor sat Brynn.

"Would you look at this!" Colin shouted, recognizing Liam from earlier in the night. "We were just talking about you! Brynn said that she came here alone, but we figured that there was no way that she could get all the way here from Graffiti Hill by herself. She probably thought we'd beat the crap outta you again, but we figured eventually you'd come looking for her!"

"And you did," his friend added as he walked behind Liam and shut the door.

"Why are you doing this?" Liam asked. "I just want my backpack. You can take the money. I don't care. I think there's probably twenty dollars left in there. I just want the rest of the stuff from it- it's important to me."

"Well, if it's important to you, maybe it's important to us too," Colin stood up and walked towards Liam, sending his mind racing as he tried to think over his options. Liam knew that there was no way Drew would be able to hear him if he shouted for him, and he knew that he did not stand a good chance of winning this fight against both of them, either. He could try to make a run for it downstairs to get Drew, bringing him back, and together, they could come to save Brynn. The only problem was that Colin's friend stood between him and the closed door, and he would have to go through him first.

Colin spoke again, "Sit down beside Brynn there, and let's go through it all together."

"Why don't you guys go downstairs and just enjoy your party?" Brynn insisted.

Liam did as he was told and sat beside Brynn while Colin pulled Liam's backpack from inside the closet.

"You see, guys, we weren't much interested in the backpack. We just took it to mess with you guys—that was until you two showed up here. We didn't think that you two would come all this way for it, but now I'm wondering why you would if there wasn't something worth something in this bag," Colin laughed, dropping the bag onto the bed. "Do you have some hidden pockets in here to hold your valuables?"

"Go ahead and check!" Liam shouted from the floor.

"You guys are going to feel pretty stupid when you see there's nothing to find," Brynn added.

Colin unzipped all the zippers and shook the bag upside down, letting everything fall onto his bed. Liam's camera fell out, crashing onto the floor. The battery compartment opened, and the batteries fell out. Liam's tin of cash, flashlight, and a couple of items of his clothing fell from the open bag as well, and lastly, from the front pocket, a sealed envelope. He then went through the items that had dropped from the backpack individually. "A flashlight," he said, trying to turn it on, "that doesn't work. A broken camera, some dork clothing, and twenty-five dollars in cash. Oh, and look at this: an envelope that just says, 'From Jacob' on it. So, tell me," Colin said, looking at the scattered items on the bed and then back to Liam, "which of these is most important to you?"

Liam looked at Brynn, who was shaking her head, and then he looked back at Colin.

"Probably the broken camera," Liam lied.

"Well, it looks like the camera is already broken, so what's the second most important thing to you?" Colin and his friend laughed at each other.

"The cash," Liam lied again.

"I don't think that's true either, Liam. You already said that I could have the cash, so it can't be why you've chased us down for your bag. I'm going to guess it's not your clothes so that just leaves the envelope," Colin lifted it in front of Liam. "Is this what's so important to you?"

Liam tried not to change any expression on his face and said nothing as the envelope hung in front of him.

"What is it? Some sort of treasure map?" Colin laughed again. "Well, if it's nothing, maybe I'll just…" Colin pulled a lighter from his pocket and held it just out of reach from the envelope. " What's in the envelope, guys?"

Again, Liam and Brynn said nothing.

"Okay, fine, have it your way," Colin said, pulling the envelope closer to the flame. Just as the fire was about to reach the paper, Brynn jumped up and grabbed it from him. Colin's friend grabbed her and held her from behind. Liam jumped up from the floor and tried to run to the door, but Colin jumped in front of him before he reached it.

"Huh, I guess there was something important about this envelope, after all."

The two pushed Liam and Brynn to the floor where they watched as Colin went to rip the envelope open. Just as he slowly began tearing the envelope's corner, the door burst open. In rushed Drew, followed in by someone else, whom Liam had guessed to be Colin's friend's older brother, whom Drew had been chatting with outside.

"Austin, Colin! What are you punks doing?" His brother called out.

Drew rushed over to Brynn and Liam, helping them up from the floor.

"Give these kids their stuff back and stop acting like a bunch of jerks!" Colin and his friend Austin loaded all of Liam's stuff back into his backpack and handed it to him. They were clearly more afraid of the older brother than the worth of tormenting Brynn and Liam any further.

Drew, Liam, and Brynn did not wait long enough to see what became of the yelling between the brothers and

Colin and left as quickly as they came in. In the car, they found Gabe asleep in the front seat.

"That is the last party I'll ever go to," Brynn announced.

"Where to now?" Drew asked once they were all inside the car again.

"Let's take Brynn home," Liam said.

"What do you mean?" Brynn asked. "We have the envelope back, we're back on track, and it's time to dig up fresh new leads!"

Liam was happy to have his backpack safely resting on his lap. But he was beyond exhausted. Nothing yet had gone to plan, and although he was feeling completely depleted, to his own surprise, he was not feeling defeated. He resolved that the mission was over. He had no more leads to follow and had no interest in putting his friends in any more danger. "No, Brynn," Liam said. "You could have gotten seriously hurt tonight, a few times now! I can't keep putting the people I care about in danger." Liam turned to the front of the car again. "Let's take Brynn home, Drew."

Chapter 20

~A Desperate Escape~

Drew knew where Brynn lived without asking, as he had been following Liam for the days since he had left home. Although Liam wanted to know all the answers to how he had managed that, he was too tired to try to ask them all now.

"You kids can drop me off anywhere around here," Gabe said.

Drew pulled over at the next block, a few streets from Brynn's house, and let Gabe out.

"I sure hope I get the chance to see you boys again," Gabe said with a soft smile.

"Thank you, Gabe," Liam smiled. "Really. Thank you for everything."

Gabe gave Liam a friendly nod and waved to them as he stepped out of the car and closed the door.

Now the three of them continued driving down the road, arriving at Brynn's house within a few minutes. Drew pulled around and parked in the back alley.

"This is where I parked while you were sleeping in that shed," Drew laughed as he put the car into park.

Brynn opened the car door and jumped out.

"I'm just going to say goodbye. Give me a few minutes," Liam said to Drew as he opened the car door and got out to meet Brynn.

"Hurry, Liam. It is a long drive home," Drew said as Liam stood with the door open, then closed it as quietly as he could.

"Brynn!" Drew called out the car window. "Do you think your parents are awake? Am I good to pull around into the driveway?"

"All the lights are out, and my mom's car wasn't in the driveway," Brynn replied. "They probably went out. They usually take my mom's car when they go anywhere together. Just park beside my stepdad's car in the driveway."

Liam stood in front of Brynn as the car pulled away. He was trying to find the words to give her the proper goodbye that she deserved. He smiled at her, wishing with every pulse of his heart that they had more time. He had grown so thankful for their friendship and was not sure what he would do now that he had to say goodbye. Although Liam knew that he did not agree with everything that she did, Liam knew that Brynn was one of the truest friends he'd ever have.

"I'm really sorry that this didn't work out the way you thought it would, Liam," she said.

"It's okay," Liam laughed reassuringly. "In a weird way, this all really helped me a lot. Not how I expected, and probably not in the way that finishing this would, but honestly, I feel better than I did on the day I first met you. I can't actually thank you enough, Brynn."

Liam watched as Brynn's eyes filled with tears. "Liam," she cried.

"Are you crying?" Liam asked.

"No! I'm not crying. I'm drowning a bug in my eye! Jeesh, Liam, I'm only human. I'm allowed to cry sometimes, too, ya know?" Brynn looked toward her dark house. "It doesn't look like my mom and Phil are home, but I have something inside that I want you to have. You can come wait in the boot room while I grab it."

Liam walked to the driveway, pointing his first finger up to Drew, implying he needed another minute more. Brynn and Liam walked into the house. "Stay here, Liam. Please don't leave this room. I'll be right back." Brynn turned away but turned back several times to make sure Liam had not moved.

He waited as patiently as he could in the boot room. He buried his hands deep in his pockets, feeling the heaviness from the weight of its contents. With all the worry over his backpack, Liam had forgotten about the cash and necklace in his jacket pocket. "Maybe there's a mailbox at the pawn shop. We can leave these on the way out of town," Liam thought. He considered placing them into his backpack, but seeing how many times it had gone missing now, he thought it best to keep them on his person.

Liam grabbed the camera from his pocket, and put it back together, hoping it still worked after it had been dropped on the floor. To his surprise, it turned on, and Liam turned around towards the door leading into the house and took a picture just to make sure it still worked, and it did. Liam looked at the picture, and on it, something on the coffee table in the next room caught his eye, sending a sick feeling to the pit of his stomach. Liam wanted to look closer at what he thought he was seeing on his camera, hoping he was wrong. Liam listened closely and could still hear Brynn walking around upstairs. Knowing it was safe to do so, he stepped outside the boot room and into the living room, taking a closer look at the table.

Liam stepped quietly, hoping that if he could sneak into the next room without Brynn knowing, all would be good. Liam felt his stomach twist when he confirmed that on the table was a handgun, as he had seen in his picture. Liam took a few more steps, and he could see that there were drugs and pills spread across the table as well. Beside the couch was a duffle bag. Liam kneeled down to peek inside. It, too, was full of drugs and another gun and the front pocket was opened, and he could see a large amount of cash. Liam had never seen drugs or guns, but even he knew that this was not an average amount for anyone to have sitting around their home, especially in their daughter's home.

"It's no wonder she's not allowed to have friends over. Brynn's parents must be drug dealers!" Liam whispered to himself, lifting his camera again and taking a picture of the table, being sure to listen for Brynn's footsteps upstairs to tell him he was still safe from being caught. Liam leaned over the coffee table, angling his camera to take a picture of the inside of the full duffle bag. At the "click" of his camera and the blink of his flash, Liam saw a terrifying face of a man in front of him, charging towards him. With a surge of fear bolting through him, Liam fell onto his back, scrambling to get back on his feet, and crawled as fast as he could away from him.

"What are you doing here?" Shouted the booming voice.

Before Liam could say anything, Brynn came running down the stairs. "Phil! This is fine. Please don't get mad. We're leaving!"

Phil's face was so twisted with anger he looked more like a bear than a human. "You aren't going anywhere! Neither of you! Brynn, who is this?!"

"This is my friend. His name is Liam. We're just leaving."

"Give me the camera, Liam," Phil took heavy steps towards Liam, stepping between him and the door. Before Phil could take another step towards him, Liam bolted towards the back door, with Brynn right behind him.

As Liam and Brynn ran out, they saw Drew in the driveway. Drew saw them running from the backyard, Phil chasing them with a baseball bat. "Drew!" Liam called as they passed him, jumping into the back seat. Drew followed them and hopped into the driver's seat, ruffling through his pockets for his keys before starting Ol' Rusty and putting the car into reverse. Although the three felt safer in the car, they would not feel truly safe until he was out of sight.

Before Drew left the driveway, Phil wound up the baseball bat and gave the front of Drew's car a hard smash, knocking the right-side light onto the driveway. Drew drove as fast as he could out of the driveway and onto the road, trying to build as much distance between them as possible before Phil could follow them. Liam looked in the rear window and realized that instead of following them, Phil began smashing his own car with the baseball bat, smashing out the backlights and bumper. Drew came to a complete stop at the first stop sign, shocked at what he was watching.

"Why is he smashing his own car?" Liam asked.

"Who cares? Drive!" Brynn yelled. As Drew drove away, Liam took his camera and quickly took some pictures of Phil smashing up the back of his car.

"Why was he doing that?" Liam asked, still shaking in the back seat. Drew did not answer. "Brynn, is he always like this?" Liam took his camera and put it back in his bag.

"No, he's not always like that. I told you to stay in the boot room! Everything would have been fine if you would have just listened to me!"

"I guess that depends on your definition of fine! Brynn, what your parents are doing is illegal, you know that."

"I know that, but she's my mom, and Phil is her husband. What am I supposed to do about it?"

"There's lots that you can do. There's no way I can let you go back to that house," Liam remarked.

"We all have screwed up situations that screw us up. I just need to give him some time to chill out, and he'll be fine. Just make sure you guys don't come by again. I'll be fine."

"Brynn," Liam said, his voice soft with concern.

"Stop, Liam. You're going too far. I'll be fine. Let's just drive around for an hour, and then you can drop me back off at home. My mom should be home by then, so she'll be able to calm Phil down."

"I'm going to pull over up here and use the pay phone to make a few calls," Drew announced as he pulled into a gas station with a pay phone outside. He grabbed a handful of quarters and jumped out.

Liam decided to drop the idea of telling Brynn that she could not return home. He understood how having a messed-up home was still better than the unknown of having nowhere to go at all. Liam looked at Brynn, his heart sinking at the thought of sending her back home. Brynn was looking out the window, and the overhead lights lit up the back seat when Liam caught a glance at a stack of papers sticking out of her pocket. He stared at it a bit longer, wondering if this was what she had gone upstairs to grab. With sudden recognition, Liam grabbed the papers from her pocket and studied them with frantic eyes.

"No, Liam, wait!" Brynn pleaded, trying to hide the tremble in her voice. "Please give those back!"

Liam thumbed his way through the papers. All were opened envelopes, all filled with letters. "From Jacob," the top one read. Liam flipped to the second. "From Jacob," he read aloud again. The same read the third, fourth, and fifth. Brynn tried to grab them back, but Liam pulled them behind his head, staring at Brynn and waiting for her to say anything.

"Brynn?" Liam finally spoke. "Where did you get these?"

"Liam, please, just listen to me," Brynn begged. "Please, just let me explain!"

"Where did you get these, Brynn?" Liam asked again, offering her a second chance to answer, his voice growing louder this time.

"Liam, I'm so sorry."

Chapter 21

~ The Mask Falls ~

It took Liam some time for his mind to catch up with everything that was happening. When it finally did, he drew in a deep breath and was sent into a dreadful state of mind as he reviewed everything that had happened in the last few days, all that they had been through, all the danger, all the lies Brynn must have told him, all the deceit, the cover-up, and the absolute disregard for anyone but herself.

"It was you all along! You're Railway Diaries! How could you do this to me?" Liam's voice cracked, but he was too angry to cry. "I trusted you. I thought you were my friend. Why didn't you just tell me?"

"I wanted to!" Brynn cried. "I was going to! I went back upstairs to grab these." She reached into her pocket, pulling the rest of the letters from her other pocket, and handed them to Liam. Each read the same, '*From Jacob,*' in his distinct handwriting. Brynn did not resist as Liam grabbed all the envelopes from her.

"I'm going to keep these," he said, his voice still sick with anger, shoving them deep into his backpack. "So you want to tell me now, but why didn't you tell me before? Why would you let me be out here chasing a ghost when it was you the entire time? Was this just all a sick game to you?"

"No, this wasn't a game to me," Brynn promised, "At first, I was scared to tell you who I was, and so I thought I could just get the letter from you without telling you, just take it from you without you even noticing. But the more I got to know you, the more I wanted to be the person you thought I could be, someone who did the right thing! You've really helped me more than you could even know, Liam. You made me feel like I could be more than I am. But the longer I waited, the more I felt like I couldn't just do the right thing. Things had gotten dangerous, and I knew you'd blame me for everything. I wanted to be better, to be like you, but that isn't me." Brynn started crying harder, which just made Liam angrier. He did not want to feel sorry for her. "I don't deserve a friend like you. I'm not like you," she said between her sobs. "I wish I was. I'd give anything to be like you. But I'm not a good person. I'm such a messed-up kid that even when I try to do the right thing, I just mess everything up!"

Liam did not have time to respond before the back seat lit up with flashing red and blue lights, and the sound of sirens drowned any chances of further discussions in the back seat. Drew dropped the phone and ran back to the car.

"We got company, guys!" Drew yelled to the back seat as he jumped into the front and pulled his car to the shoulder of the road.

Liam looked out the back window to see if the police car would pull up behind them; it did and then parked. The sirens were off now, but the blue and red lights remained behind them. Liam turned back to Brynn; his face still sharp with anger.

"They'll take you home, Liam. You're a wanted man, remember?" Brynn said, but Liam did not say anything back. "I'm sorry," Brynn said again as she reached her arm out to Liam, ripping his backpack from his hands. Then she jumped out of the car with it, slamming the door behind her.

Liam went to follow her, but by the time he had removed his seatbelt and opened the car door, Brynn had disappeared into the night unnoticed by the officers.

The police officer saw him and yelled. "Stay in the car! Close the door!" Liam did as he was told and closed the door quickly. The two officers walked slowly up to the brothers, writing down the license plate number. Then they both walked to the front of the vehicle, taking a closer look at the damaged front and missing headlight.

"Step out of the vehicle, please," the first officer said, shining his flashlight into Drew's window.

"What's the problem, officer?" Drew asked

"I said to step out of the vehicle, now!" Drew and Liam did not risk the officer having to tell them a third time, and both jumped out of the car with hands raised far above their heads. The second officer pushed Drew against the car, patting him down before he handcuffed him.

"What are you doing? What do you think he did?" Liam asked. Looking up, he realized that it was Officer Douglas handcuffing Drew.

"We'll ask the questions here," the officer snapped back, turning his attention to Liam. "Ah, I recognize you from the train yard the other day! I thought I told you to stay out of trouble!" Officer Douglas' partner then pushed Liam against the car and patted him down. "What's this in your pocket?" The officer asked, patting down Liam's jacket. Is there anything in here that could poke, stab, or hurt me?"

"No, I don't have a weapon," Liam replied, "it's just a neckla.." Liam swallowed hard to silence himself.

"Look at this. It looks like you boys are in for a long night," the officer said, pulling the plastic bag out of Liam's pocket and opening it to find it full of cash and the gold necklace. "We got you for a hit-and-run, and I have to check at the station to be sure, but this looks an awful lot like a necklace that was stolen from the pawn shop just up the road from here."

"No! You got this all wrong. This is not what it looks like," Liam pleaded.

"If I had a nickel for every time I'd heard that, I could have been happily retired a long time ago," Officer Douglas replied, just as stone-faced as he had in the train yard.

It was clear to Liam that it was too late to plead. The brothers were now both cuffed and lowered into the back of the police car, and a tow truck was ordered to bring Ol' Rusty down to the station.

Liam and Drew were silent as the officers drove them to the station. The officers did not speak much to each other, and other than the two-way radio going off every few minutes, the drive was quiet. Once the brothers were taken from the back of the police car and brought inside, they were separated and towed down opposite hallways. "Let my brother go. He didn't do anything!" Liam could hear Drew shouting, watching as he struggled to get out of the handcuffs as he was shuffled down the hall.

Liam did not know what to expect as he was walked down the hallway, his arms still bound behind him in the metal cuffs that were now beginning to bruise his wrists. Officer Douglas's hand was grasped tight on the back of his arm. At first, he thought that maybe the room he was being led to would be dark, and the only light would be a poorly lit lamp on the table. Perhaps it would be dank and cold, where he'd be questioned and roughed up by people unknown, like the interrogation rooms he'd seen in movies. But he was wrong.

Officer Douglas took him into a simple room. It was pretty warm, with a carpeted floor, a table, and three chairs, all in view from the good amount of light from the ceiling fixtures. Officer Douglas sat Liam down in one of the chairs, uncuffed him, and then left the room. As Liam looked around, but he did not even feel how he expected to. Liam was not sure if it was all the danger he had faced in the last few days or if it was all the time he had spent with Brynn McFarlay that had made him braver. It could have been that he was so tired that he no longer cared, but as he sat alone in the room, he found that he was not nervous or scared at all; mostly, he felt annoyed. Liam sat in that chair, resting his head on his arms, and waited for over an hour before the door opened again.

Walking in was Officer Douglas, and in his hand, tucked away in a bag marked "evidence," was the necklace and in another was the cash. Officer Douglas put both bags on the table in front of Liam and watched his face for a reaction. "Well, it's been confirmed. This is the stolen necklace from Pat's Pawnshop. So, I guess our only question for you is if you and your brother were working together on this or if it was just your brother? Not only do we have you for the necklace and cash, but you were apprehended in a vehicle with damages that match a vehicle from a hit-and-run not too far from where we found you, and the owner called in a vehicle matching your brother's vehicle description. So, with all that, I suggest that you start talking."

Liam sat quietly, listening to the accusations being thrown at him. Liam knew the truth was just as simple as an explanation. He had spent years watching his brothers and their mischievous and trouble-making ways. He thought if he could just harness even a bit of their confidence, he'd be able to explain everything in perfect sense to Officer Douglas and get them out of this mess in no time.

"I know how this looks, and I doubt you'll believe me, but this seriously is not what it seems. I did not steal this stuff. Someone I know did. I was just holding onto it until we could return it."

"So, you're saying that your brother stole it?" Officer Douglas accused.

"What? No!" Liam shouted.

Officer Douglas inched his chair across the floor and closer to the table. "So, you expect me to believe that you were just caught before you could do the right thing?"

"On my honor!" Liam replied.

"Ah yes, the honor of a thief! Doesn't hold much weight around here, I'm afraid."

Liam was getting more frustrated by the minute. None of this was going according to plan, and he felt like the more he spoke, the more Officer Douglas used it against him, "Listen to me, it wasn't my brother. It was someone else. As for the damage to the vehicle, I saw something I shouldn't have. Drugs, and guns, and money. The owner who said we damaged his car is a drug dealer. Now he's trying to set us up! This man smashed up my brother's car and then smashed up his own car! I got pictures of all this. You just have to believe me!"

"You have pictures of all of this? Where?"

"Yes! They're on my camera!"

"And where is this camera?"

"It's in my backpack, which was stolen when you pulled us over!"

Officer Douglas looked at Liam, his eyes narrowed skeptically. He said nothing for a moment, then pushed a piece of paper and pen in front of Liam. "Here," Officer Douglas said, "write out your statement. Don't leave out a single detail."

Liam did as he was instructed, in almost every detail. The only thing he left out was Brynn's name. Once Liam was finished, Officer Douglas got up and left the room again, the statement in hand. He was gone for about thirty minutes. Liam figured he had left him alone so long to stew in his own nerves. But not today. Liam was all out of nerves to stew in. After some time, Liam heard the footsteps as Officer Douglas walked up to the door, opening it and closing it again before sitting back in his chair.

"Well, Liam!" Officer Douglas said, slapping a piece of paper in front of him. His face, in black and white print, was on the paper, staring back at him, with big bold letters, *"Missing"* written across the top. Liam did not react. "So let me see if I understand your statement, Liam. What you're saying happened is that someone you know who is not your brother stole the cash and necklace and gave it to you to hold on to until you could return it to the store?" Officer Douglas paused while flipping to the next page of the written statement, "and when you saw something that you shouldn't have seen, examples given: drugs, guns and obvious signs of drug dealing, someone smashed the front light of your brother's car before taking the baseball bat and smashing his own car so he could call it into the police before you could so you would be less credible to us?"

"I told you that you weren't going to believe me," Liam huffed, crossing his arms over his chest defensively.

"Would you believe a story like that? You gotta do better than that if you want me to believe you," Officer Douglas knitted his fingers together and leaned towards Liam, "I want to help you here, kid, I really do, but you gotta give me something more to work with."

"I'm not lying to you. This is exactly what happened! Go and ask my brother. He'll tell you the same thing!"

"Just sit tight, Liam," Officer Douglas rose from his seat again. "I'll be back." Liam sat alone in the room again, wondering how he would escape the mess he had created. He eventually stopped watching the clock as another hour went by, totaling Liam's time in that room to four hours so far and with no hope of an end in sight. After a while longer, a knock at the door caused Liam to sit straight up. He expected to see the stern face of Officer Douglas frowning at him as he found his seat, demanding a new story for Liam to defend.

Instead, to his surprise, two familiar, smiling faces walked through the door, sending a surge of warmth through Liam's tired and aching body.

Chapter 22

~ Old Friends, New Friends ~

& New Beginnings

Liam stood to his feet as quickly as they could lift him. "Gabe! Brynn! I didn't think you'd come!" Brynn walked slowly in the door behind Gabe. Behind her, Officer Douglas walked in.

"I didn't think I would either," Brynn admitted. "But if there's one thing I've learned from you, it's that it's never too late to do the right thing."

Liam smiled with his entire face as he rushed over to Brynn and pulled her in for a tight hug with both arms. Brynn buried her face into Liam's shoulder, tears from her eyes soaking into his jacket.

"Miss McFarlay has told us everything and both your stories match up," Officer Douglas announced, still standing in the doorway. "She's shown us the pictures on your camera and has taken the blame for stealing the necklace and cash. I've given Ms. Patty from the pawn shop a call, and she has said she does not wish to press charges."

Liam saw Drew walk in from behind the officer. Liam ran to his brother and hugged him, both breathing a sigh of relief. The smiles written on their faces read that they shared the same happiness. "There's someone in the hallway who wants to come in and see you, too," Drew smiled and turned back to the front door. "Come in!"

There was nothing that could have prepared Liam, and he felt his own heart nearly jump out of his chest at the comfort the man at the door brought him. "Mr. Lister!" Liam cried out, running to hug him. "How did you even know to come here!?"

"I reported you missing!" Mr. Lister explained. "I've been looking everywhere for you boys, and when the police found you and were holding you here, they called me since I was the one who had made the report." Mr. Lister pulled both of the brothers in for another hug, belly laughing with joy to be reunited with them again.

"I didn't see my face on the news," Drew laughed.

"Well, my boy, they said you were too old for me to report missing and told me I was worrying about nothing. But I pressed them, and finally, they took my report about Liam here, being that he's underage, and I figured you two would be together."

"Thanks for coming for us!" Liam pulled in closer for a hug.

"You're coming home with me. You're both coming to live with me. I promise we'll get your father the help that he needs, but until then, you are coming to live with me!"

"Are you sure?" Liam asked. "Can we really?"

"Absolutely, my boys!" Mr. Lister replied with a reassuring smile.

"Thank you!" Liam could hardly fathom all that had happened. His heart quite literally was jumping as he tried to.

"I'm just sorry I didn't take you boys in sooner," Mr. Lister admitted, pulling Liam in by his shoulder. Liam looked over Mr. Lister's face and could see the pain he was trying to hide, recognizing it as the same guilt that he, himself, had been carrying around since Jacob's death. Liam smiled at Mr. Lister but said nothing. Someday soon, he knew that he would share all that Gabe had shared with him, and he hoped that it would help Mr. Lister let go of the guilt so he could heal, too. But not today. Today was for celebrating, and Liam was in a room full of almost all of his favourite people.

The entire room was busy with laughter, but beside him, Liam noticed as Officer Douglas pulled Brynn aside. "I'm sorry, Brynn. We can't let you go home after the pictures you showed us," the officer said with a sympathetic look. "We'll be doing a house call to your family, but for now, social services are on their way. Do you have any close family members you want me to call?"

"I have an aunt. Do you think I'll be able to stay with her?" Brynn asked.

"I'll see what I can do, Brynn." The officer smiled, patting Brynn on the back of her shoulder as she joined back with the others.

"Oh, before I forget," Mr. Lister reached deep into his pant pocket. "There was an elderly lady in the hallway a few minutes ago. She asked me to give these to you both." From his pocket, Mr. Lister retrieved two three-leaf clover pendants. Liam grabbed them in excitement, recognizing them as the same as Mrs. Patty had shown them in her store.

Attached was a sticky note that read:

"Dear children, remember, always have faith, hope, and love."

Liam and Brynn smiled at each other as they pinned their three-leaf clovers to their sweaters. The others in the room wondered what was so meaningful about these pendants, but no one asked.

"Gabe!" Liam called to the back of the room where Gabe was standing quietly on his own. "I want you to meet Mr. Lister."

Mr. Lister shook Gabe's hand with excitement like an old friend seeing him after a long departure. "Drew was telling me out in the hallway that you're a little down on your luck. I know of some resources in Larsen Creek that can help you get back onto your feet. If you're interested, I'm sure I could pull a few strings to even bring those resources here to Boulder Ridge so you don't have to relocate."

Gabe thanked Mr. Lister and offered his hand for another shake. "I appreciate it, but we all have a purpose, and we should do it on purpose. I'm happy living where I am, but please know that I appreciate the offer."

Mr. Lister smiled at Gabe respectfully. "If you ever change your mind or need help, please contact me."

Gabe nodded with a gracious smile and went to walk towards the door, waving as he walked.

"Gabe!" Liam called, running after him before he made it out the door. "Why don't you take the help? You can have a home again. You won't have to always wonder where your next meal is coming from. You've helped me more than you'll ever know. Please, let us help you now."

"That may all be true, Liam. But who knows, if I had a home now, maybe I would never have met you kids. There may be more people out there who need help from someone like me, and I want to be out there if they do."

Liam had no argument for that. "I really can't thank you enough," Liam smiled. Gabe kindly smiled back at the boy and walked out the door, giving the room a big wave of his arm as he left.

Liam turned back and looked around the room. Drew was talking to Mr. Lister, and Brynn was walking over to him, lifting his backpack up. "The police said they need to keep your camera until they're done with their investigation."

Liam took his backpack but did not know what to say to her.

"I'm really sorry for ditching you back there, Liam."

"It's all good. I'm just so glad you came back when you did."

"So am I," Brynn admitted. "I didn't open the envelope, and I left every letter your brother ever sent me in there."

Liam reached into the front pocket of his backpack, grabbing the still-sealed envelope of the last letter Jacob had ever written. "This is for you," Liam smiled as he handed it to her.

Brynn flashed red as she took the envelope. *'From Jacob'* she read as she turned the envelope over to open it. Slowly, she unfolded the letter, read the first line, and looked up at Liam, her eyes gleaming with happiness as they filled with tears. "This letter isn't for me, Liam," Brynn paused as she folded the letter back up. "It's for you."

"What?!" Liam took the letter and unfolded it as quickly as he could. He tried to focus his eyes enough to even read the first on the paper held in his shaking hands. He read the first line aloud, *"Dear Liam."* Liam held the letter close to his heart, and his eyes quickly filled with tears. He continued reading.

"Dear Liam," he read again,

"I must have written this letter to you a thousand times. I'm sorry that I'm leaving without saying goodbye to you. I want to thank you for always being such a wonderful brother. I wish that I could see the world the way you do. I love you so much,

Love always,

Jacob

Liam folded the letter and placed it back into the envelope. Liam felt a warmth spread over his body, and more tears formed in the corner of his eyes.

Brynn hugged Liam. "I'm so glad that he wrote you this letter, Liam. After seeing how far you'd go for him, I know he knew how much you loved him."

Liam reached into his backpack again, handing Brynn all the envelopes Jacob had ever written her.

"Are you sure, Liam?" Brynn asked, taking them in her hand.

"Yes, of course," Liam confirmed. "I've got my own."

"Come on, Liam," Mr. Lister called, having no idea about the letter. "It's very early in the morning, and we can't stay in this room all day. They need it to interrogate the real criminals!"

Liam laughed, and he and Brynn followed Drew and Mr. Lister out of the room. Brynn walked with Liam to the front door and waited as Mr. Lister and Drew pulled the cars around front.

"Officer Douglas has called my aunt. She said she'd take me in. He's told me to wait here for her and the social worker to finish talking."

"So, I guess that this is goodbye then?" Liam sighed.

"I guess so," Brynn answered. "But I was thinking about it and wanted to ask you. Do you want to be pen pals?"

Liam smiled warmly and nodded his head. Brynn wrote down her aunt's
address.

"You'd better write me, Liam Robertson. But let's use the post office. Mailing them will be easier than sending them by train!"

Liam laughed and agreed. Out front, Liam heard Mr. Lister and Drew honking their horns at him. Liam waved at them and turned back to Brynn. "Well, I'll be seeing you around, I'm sure of it." Liam gave Brynn one last hug. "Take care of yourself, Barley."

Brynn smiled, wrapping her arms tighter around Liam. "You take care of yourself too, Chicken Legs."